'These stories [illegible] very id[illegible] exists. In Bed[illegible] fictiona[illegible] attitudes are suspect. To be huma[illegible] damaged is to be human.'

JAMES ROBERTSON

'These short stories are full of surprising twists and unexpected outcomes. They are rooted in everyday experience, but take the reader on a journey through other people's lives as seen from their unique viewpoints.'

MATTHEW BRADBY, QUEEN'S NURSING INSTITUTE

AWARDS FOR BEDA HIGGINS' WRITING

WINNER: Northern Writer Award 2010
WINNER: Mslexia short story competition 2009
WINNER: Residential Prize, Biscuit publishing 2007
WINNER: Northern Promise Award 2004

LONGLIST: Edgehill Prize 2012

SHORTLIST: Luke Bitmead Novel Award shortlist 2012
SHORTLIST: Cinnamon Press novel Award 2010
SHORTLIST: Novel Lit Idol national competition 2004

READ REGIONAL RECOMMENDATION 2011

Also by Beda Higgins

SHORT STORY COLLECTION

Chameleon

POEMS AND STORIES IN ANTHOLOGIES

Root

Grist

Biscuit Publishing

Bloodaxe

Ten by Ten Press

Id on Tyne Press

Literary and Philosophical National Poetry

STORIES IN OTHER PUBLICATIONS

Mslexia

Alpha to Omega Tyne Wear

Little Crackers

tales from the edge

beda higgins

Saraband

Published by Saraband,
Suite 202, 98 Woodlands Road
Glasgow, G3 6HB, Scotland
www.saraband.net

ISBN: 9781908643681
ebook: 9781908643698

Printed in the EU on sustainably sourced paper.

Editor: Craig Hillsley
Text design: Laura Jones

1 3 5 7 9 10 8 6 4 2

For Bernard, Rachel, Joe and Tom

'Pity the man who is not wounded,
who doesn't feel wounded by life'
JAMES WRIGHT

Contents

arthur's last adventure

'Gracious me, you gave me quite a start,' Arthur said. 'Why are you under a park bench?'

'I'm hiding,' the small boy whispered. 'Pretend you haven't seen me, my cousin's coming.'

Arthur watched an older, thickset boy stomping up the path. He was whacking blooms off the flowers with a stick. Once the boy had gone round the corner, Arthur peeped under the bench. 'It's all clear. Do come out, you must be terribly uncomfortable down there.'

The small boy crawled out; he was covered in mud. 'My cousin pushed me in a ditch.' He sniffed and wiped his nose using his sleeve.

Arthur took a clean linen handkerchief from his jacket pocket and offered it to the boy, who shook his head. 'I've decided to run away.'

'Run away? Should I be running, too?' Arthur looked alarmed.

'No, you're a grown-up.' The boy wrinkled his nose. 'What would you need to run away from?'

'Oh, you'd be surprised.' Arthur raised an eyebrow.

'I'm running away from everything,' the boy said, waving his arms.

'Everything? That's an awful lot to run away from.'

'Mainly my brother, except I don't think Steven really is my brother. I hate him.' The boy slumped down on the grass, scowling.

Arthur lowered himself slowly to sit on the bench, whistling lightly through his teeth. He rested his hands on his knees. His skin was patterned in liver spots and wormy veins.

The boy looked at Arthur's hands. 'How old are you?'

'I'm very old. But there's life in the old dog yet.' He straightened his tie and cleared his throat. 'Tell me, how long do you intend to run away for?'

The boy shrugged. 'Until I'm a grown-up and can leave home properly.'

Arthur concentrated on filling his pipe. He didn't smoke nowadays, but liked the meticulous ritual of getting it ready. It gave him something to do.

The boy rubbed his face, a patch of pink glowed under the caked-on mud. 'This itches.' He looked across the park. 'If I go now, they won't know I've run away until later. Mum lets me play out with my cousin all day, as long as I'm back by teatime.'

'Why do you hate your big brother?'

'He's gross.' He dug his toe into a rut in the grass and pushed down hard.

'Why?'

'He's mental. He's got something wrong with him. He acts like a baby even though he's huge. He's all cross-eyed and his teeth stick out, and he laughs at the top of his voice at nothing and waves his arms all over the place.'

'Oh dear.'

'I'm sick of being the freak's brother – that's what they call him.'

'Who calls him that?'

'My cousin, the kids at school. That's what he is – a freak.' He kicked a sod of earth.

Arthur looked over his glasses. 'Oh dear. We can choose our friends, but we're stuck with our family.'

The boy stood up, twitching and scratching. 'He smells too, and he's always putting his hands down his pants. I hate being his brother.' He stomped round the bench.

Arthur watched the boy circling. He was small and wiry under his filthy, baggy clothes. 'Where are you running to?' Arthur asked.

'My dad.'

'Won't he be at your house?'

'No, he's in America. I'll have to catch a plane.'

'I think you'll find you need a passport to get on a plane.'

The boy thought about this and clicked his fingers. 'I know – I'll get a boat. I could be a stowaway, couldn't I?' His eyes shone, embedded in mud. 'I've decided this is the start of my new life.' He lifted his arms triumphantly. 'Stupid Steven's ruined my life here, so I'm going to make a new one. I got the idea from a programme my mum watches. It's about people having new lives in new countries because they're fed up of the ones they have here. I won't be smelly Steven's brother anymore. I'll just be me – Peter, normal Peter.'

'Won't your dad wonder why you came alone when you arrive in America?'

'What do you mean?'

'Won't he wonder where your mother and Steven are?'

'No. It was Steven that made my dad leave in the first place. He left when he was four and I was just born. It was because Steven is special, that's why my dad ran away, and now I'm running away, too. I used to be cross about it, but now I'm older and I understand.' He held his chin high.

Arthur looked at him. 'You know, I don't think they'll let you on a boat to America quite so dirty. They're fussy about germs, the Americans.'

Peter rubbed his eyes. The mud was drying fast and cracking. 'I've thought about that and I'm going to jump in the park fountain at the entrance once everyone's gone. I've got a polythene bag under my bed at home. It's got clean clothes and a whole packet of Kit Kats. I'll sneak back and get it. I've had it ready for a while because I've been thinking of running away for a while.'

Arthur nodded. 'You clearly have a well-thought-out plan. I admire that.' He got out an old-fashioned stopwatch from the inside of his tweed jacket.

Peter looked at it. 'That's a fancy watch. I know all about watches and how they work and stuff.'

'You are clearly a bright young man.'

Peter gave his first smile. 'My teacher, Mr Snowdon, says I'm clever. He knows I'm completely different from Steven.' His eyes narrowed. 'I wish he'd say it out loud to the whole class so Mark Williams could hear. I'm sick of him.' Peter kicked the ground again. 'He makes me want to run away, too. He calls me spakka because I'm Steven's brother.'

'That's not fair at all,' Arthur said, shaking his head. 'It seems to me part of the problem generally in life is that people don't like anyone who's a bit different, who doesn't conform.'

Peter wiped his nose. 'I don't know what you mean.'

Arthur wound his watch. 'Don't you think Steven should be allowed to live his life in peace even though he may act oddly?'

'No, he's really annoying. You'd want to run away if you lived with him. I can't have friends round – he puts them off their dinners, dribbling and eating with his mouth open and full of mush. He makes my mum tired. She has to keep changing his bed.' Peter was circling the bench again, glowering.

Arthur watched him; he was a feisty little man. Arthur rubbed his chin. 'Do you know, as you've been talking, I've been thinking? I live alone in a big house and I wander room to room, dawn to dusk. I go upstairs and downstairs and I really don't know what to do with myself. I used to spend a lot of time tinkering in my cellar, but nowadays I simply can't be bothered. Quite frankly, Peter, I'm lonely. I've been thinking as you've been telling me about running away, what a wonderful adventure you'll have. Have you ever been to America?'

'No.'

'Oh, it's marvellous, I used to work there. I was an FBI agent.' Arthur sat forward a little, his old eyes sparkling. 'We had such fun catching spies and stopping madcap scientists from taking over the world, and pitting our wits against villainous evil enemies.'

'What, a bit like 007?'

'Very like 007.' Arthur tapped the side of his nose. 'Between you and me, Peter' – he dropped his voice and pointed to his chest – 'I am 006.'

'Really?' His eyes widened.

'Oh yes, but please keep it to yourself. Secret agent stuff needs to be kept secret,' he said with a wink.

'I won't tell anyone.'

'So I was thinking – but this is only a suggestion, I understand completely if you don't agree with my idea – why don't I come with you?'

'What, to America?'

'Exactly. You wouldn't have to stay with me at all, of course, once we got there. You could go and find your father, and I think I would head for California. I like the sunshine and I've always liked the sea. I've heard the Californian waves are wonderful.'

'Is that near Disneyland?'

'Yes, I do believe it is.'

'I'd like to go there.'

Arthur smiled. 'You could always come to Disneyland and then go on and find your father. Do you know whereabouts in America he is?'

'Not really.'

'It may be that my contacts in the FBI can help you out there.'

'That would be good,' said Peter, 'except I don't know what he looks like nowadays.'

'I'm sure it won't be a problem. There are all sorts of clever ways of finding people nowadays. Believe me,' Arthur said, chuckling, 'I ought to know.'

'It'd be great to see my dad, my real dad.'

'There are only real dads, aren't there?'

'Yeah, s'pose, but Mum has this boyfriend, who calls me "son" – I hate him, too.'

'Oh dear. I do believe an adventure would do you the world of good, Peter. Travelling on the boat would be much easier to do with me there. You can be my grandson and we'll tell everyone we're having a trip of a lifetime to Disneyland. Otherwise, you'll have to hide in the lifeboat for the whole journey, and I don't know what you'd do when you need the toilet.'

Peter thought about it.

'Also, I could drive us to the dock to catch the boat. I still have my 006 car, you see. They let me keep it.'

'Is it like 007's?'

'Yes, very. Lots of gadgets and what-not.'

'Do you have an ejector seat and everything?'

Arthur nodded. 'Ejector seat, exhaust guns, laser beam headlights, spiked wheels, and fire-spurting gaskets. There's really very little difference between James Bond's and my car.'

'It sounds mint.' Peter rubbed his face again.

Arthur reached for his walking stick and hit it on the ground gently. 'See this walking stick?'

Peter nodded.

'It has a poisonous dart at the end. If I swivel the handle here at the top, it shoots out. Whoever it hits is dead before they hit the floor.'

Peter grinned. 'Cool.'

Arthur picked his hat up and patted it on his head. 'One can't be too careful nowadays, what with muggers and thieves around, especially in a park.'

Peter looked at Arthur. 'I'd never have thought, looking at you…'

'Oh Peter, one of life's most important lessons is that looks can be deceiving. Take your mother's boyfriend, for example; I'm sure he looks a perfectly pleasant young man, but of course you know differently.' Arthur emptied his pipe and slipped it into the top pocket of his jacket. 'First things first, I think. People will notice you looking so dirty. The last thing you want when you're running away is to get noticed.'

Peter looked down at his filthy clothes and sniffed. 'They smell, too. My mum'll go nuts. She always says it's my fault even when it's not.'

'Why don't you pop back to my house with me? I've lots of hot water and fluffy towels. After a bath, you could put your fresh clothes on. You can even take some of my nephews' if you want.'

'Are they my age?'

'Oh yes – always your age.'

It was getting cloudy; Peter shivered. 'Okay, that sounds good.'

Arthur heaved himself forward to stand. He rummaged in his pocket and pulled out some keys. He peered over his glasses, muttering, 'Front door… cellar… back door. Righty-ho, all present and correct.'

'Which way?' Peter asked.

Arthur put his hand on Peter's neck. 'I'll show you.' His knees ached and his hands were gnarled with arthritis, but he felt the warmth of that lovely, young skin warming his bones. He stroked the curving nave of the small, thin neck before moving his hand to the boy's shoulder, gripping slightly. 'Oh, I'm too old for adventures nowadays, Peter. But I think this one last time, eh?'

the cough

Dr Simon cycled to work. He was doing his GP rotation in an inner city practice. He wanted to do good, to make a difference. At dinner parties he sipped wine and grazed the cheeseboard while speaking fervently about social inequalities.

He buzzed his next patient in. It was fourteen-month-old Charlene again. He glanced at the baby's fifteen-year-old mother pushing the buggy.

'She's still coughing loads,' said Carly.

'Let's have a look at her, shall we?'

'My mum was wondering if she should see a specialist.'

'Why?'

'She says in case there's something seriously wrong with her.'

Dr Simon folded his stethoscope and sat down. 'She's got a bit of an upper respiratory tract infection – in other words, a cough. It'll go with time. There's still no need for antibiotics, it's probably viral.' Dr Simon smiled. 'She's on the plump side, isn't she?'

'She's always hungry,' said Carly.

'If people – even babies – get fat, it can make it harder for them to breathe. Try not feeding her every time she cries.'

Carly bit her lip. 'I'll try.'

Dr Simon sent a note to the health visitor to do a home visit for Charlene. Talk about feeding.

A few weeks later, Carly sat opposite Dr Simon again. She had her hair tied up in a neat ponytail and was wearing a pretty knee-length skirt. Baby Charlene was in a pink, teddy bear two-piece with a ribbon in her thin hair.

Dr Simon smiled. 'Charlene looks very pretty today. Well done, Carly.'

She blushed. 'I like to keep her looking nice.'

'What's the problem?' he asked.

'She cries and coughs all night. My mum's getting fed up of her always crying.'

'How old is she now?'

'Fifteen months.'

'Is she walking?'

'No.'

'If she was doing a bit more,' said Dr Simon, 'it'd be better for her cough. Try and play with her. Get her out of the buggy and roll around on the floor with her.'

'What d 'you mean?'

'Roll about and crawl – see if she'll copy you. She needs to get used to movement and using her body. Stand her up and see if she'll weight-bear, start encouraging her to walk.'

Carly raised an eyebrow. 'I'll try, Dr Simon, but it's hard cos I'm waiting for a council house and I'm trying to keep her as quiet as I can. Everyone's already narky with me at home with her waking up at night coughing. I have to give her a bottle then to settle her.'

'I understand that, Carly, but you're making a rod for your own back.'

'Eh?'

'It means you're getting into bad habits. If you give in to her every time, she'll expect to be fed every time she wakes.' He looked at baby Charlene. With each visit to the surgery she was ballooning.

'I'll try and play with her then,' she said, nodding earnestly.

Dr Simon opened the door for her.

'Thanks, doctor.' Carly beamed. She had a big gap between her teeth.

He watched her push the buggy, tottering on high platforms. She walked like a child dressing up in her mother's shoes.

The next week, the receptionist dropped some notes on his table. 'I think our little Carly has a crush on you. She's here again, insisting she'll only see you.'

'She's still coughing and she's dribbling loads,' said Carly.

'It's probably her teeth,' said Dr Simon. 'You know, Carly, you can ring the health visitor about this sort of thing.'

Her eyes widened. 'But I trust you.'

He smiled. 'What about you, Carly, do you have any plans for the future?'

'I'm gonna look after Charlene.'

'Good for you, but have you thought about going back to college?'

'No,' she said, shaking her head, 'I don't want to go there.'

'I wouldn't rule it out altogether, Carly. I'm sure you're a clever girl and could get a good job with some qualifications.'

Carly perked up. 'I'd quite like to be a beautician.'

'Why don't you look into what exams you need to pass to become one? You could have a proper career.'

A few days later, Carly was back, this time with her mother. Carly looked embarrassed and sulky. 'She's been worse this week, coughing all night.' She glanced at her mother and bit her nails.

Charlene obligingly gave a chewy cough. Dr Simon looked at Charlene. She was pale, wan and asleep.

'Does she normally sleep in the daytime?'

'Oh yeah, for hours and hours.'

'That's probably why she's not sleeping at night. You need to keep her awake in the daytime.'

'I don't think we're getting to the bottom of the problem,' said Carly's mum, folding her arms. 'Carly's been bringing her down here for weeks, and she still has a cough.'

Dr Simon noticed her tattoo. He took an instant dislike to her. He bent down and unwrapped the blanket Charlene was swaddled in; it smelt like an old ashtray. He frowned. 'Do you smoke, Carly?'

'No, never, but Mam does.'

'I never smoke near our Charlene.' The mother stuck her chin out defiantly. 'I'd never do that, I'm really strict about it.'

'Carly, I'll need you to lift Charlene up so I can listen to her back.' He spoke pointedly to Carly, ignoring her mother.

Carly awkwardly bent down and gently lifted up her baby.

'She must be getting heavy for you,' he said.

'You're a heffalump, aren't you, babes?' said Carly sweetly to Charlene.

'All my children are big-boned, nothing wrong with that,' the mother said brusquely.

'As I said to Carly in one of her previous visits, Charlene would be a lot healthier if she was more active.'

The mother sighed impatiently. 'Don't tell me – tell Carly. She's meant to be the one looking after her, but she's got her head in the clouds. The latest is she's going to do a beautician course.' She turned on Carly, raising her voice. 'She's your baby, not mine. I've done my bit. I'm not going to do it a second time round.'

Dr Simon and Carly's eyes met briefly.

Charlene groggily cried as if to remind them why they were there. Her eyes barely opened.

Dr Simon listened to Charlene's chest carefully. He folded his stethoscope and sighed. 'She does seem to have an infection.'

'So after all these sleepless weeks,' Carly's mum snapped, 'you're telling us she can have antibiotics now?'

'Mam, don't,' said Carly quietly.

'I told you,' she said, wagging her finger. 'Didn't I tell you, Carly, to see one of the other doctors? We've had all those sleepless nights and now he'll do us a big favour and give us the medicine.' Her eyes narrowed. 'How long have you been a doctor? Are you a proper doctor or one of them students?'

'Mrs Bain, I can assure you I am a proper doctor. Your granddaughter didn't need antibiotics last week; it was a virus. If you abuse antibiotics by overusing them, you'll develop a resistance. The cough's probably been exacerbated – I mean, made worse – by someone smoking near her. Cigarette smoke is very harmful to infants.'

'How dare you!' she flared. 'Are you suggesting I'd smoke near my granddaughter? This is bloody ridiculous.' She stood and zipped up her bomber jacket. 'It's a complete waste of time. You don't know how to make her better so you're blaming me for her cough.' She shook her head. 'Come on, you,' she said to Carly. 'And next time, make sure you see a proper doctor,' she sneered as she left. 'Not one who's still learning.'

Carly's cheeks burned. She turned at the door and mouthed *sorry* before scurrying out after her mother. As the door shut behind them, Dr Simon heard Carly say feebly, 'He *is* a proper doctor, Mam.'

His heart sank when he saw Charlene's name on his list the following week. He checked the health visitor's report. *Home circumstances are chaotic but there is no indication child protection procedures need to be implemented. Carly is a young inexperienced mum but does appear to care here for baby. She also has the support of the maternal grandmother.*

Dr Simon met Dr Brown, the senior partner, in the corridor. He ran the case past him. 'I don't seem to be getting anywhere with her. It's always a cough, which I'm sure is due to lack of activity and the grandmother smoking near her. Her blanket stank of stale cigarettes. Carly's just a kid herself, and the grandmother seems intent on grinding the poor girl's confidence down.'

Dr Brown patted his arm. 'There'll be plenty more Carlys in your career, Simon. My advice is to do what you can with the least fuss. Get in and get out, you can't save the world. For the likes of Charlene, you have to lower your standards. We're doing a good job if she doesn't come to any real harm. History repeats itself; have you ever wondered how old Carly's mum was when she had Carly? My bet is she'll have been about fifteen, too.'

'But her smoking near the baby, surely that's some kind of neglect? Particularly as Charlene seems to be a child prone to coughs.'

Dr Brown shrugged. 'We can tell them what to do, but in people's own homes, they are the boss.'

'I'm sure Carly's a bright kid, if she could just get away from her mother.'

'Simon, don't get involved.' He shook his head. 'It's not worth it. You'll wear yourself out.'

The following week, Dr Simon groaned. 'Not again.'

Carly looked nervous. 'I've had to sneak out. Mam says I can't see you anymore. She says... Oh, it doesn't matter what she says.' She blushed. 'I know you're a good doctor and I'm dead worried about Charlene.' She bit her lip. 'There's something not right with her.'

Dr Simon looked at Charlene. Her breathing was laboured. She was sweaty and flushed. He listened to her chest. Again the smell of cigarette smoke clung to her blanket. He was furious. He kept his voice level and spoke quietly. 'Carly, you have to keep any cigarette smokers away from Charlene, and that includes your mother. The fumes are damaging her lungs.'

Carly nodded with her head down. 'I'll try.'

'I know it must be difficult for you.'

She nodded. 'It is.'

'Have you heard when you might be getting your council flat?'

'No, I'm still too far down the list,' she said wearily.

Dr Simon wrote out a prescription for more antibiotics. He thought about what Dr Brown had said. He needed to ensure that Charlene didn't come to harm. 'She must take these antibiotics regularly, and I want you to try really hard to play with her more. And, Carly, will you try and keep her with you at all times next week? That way you can make sure no one smokes near her.'

'I will, doctor, I promise I will.'

'Good girl.'

She gave her gap-toothed grin. 'Thanks, Dr Simon.'

At home, Carly told her mum, 'I saw Dr Brown; he's given me more antibiotics.'

'Well, I'm glad you saw him and not that tosser. I hope these are the right pills to make her better this time.' She looked at Charlene. 'Poor little mite.' She reached down to lift her out of the buggy. 'How's my princess?' she cooed.

'It's alright, I'll mind her, Mam.' Carly avoided looking at her mother as she slipped round and unclipped Charlene, heaving her onto her shoulder. 'I'll take her up to my room.'

Her mum raised an eyebrow and put her hands on her hips. 'Good. It's about time you started looking after her.'

Carly hummed as she went upstairs. She shut her bedroom door and placed Charlene carefully in the middle of the bed so she couldn't roll off. Carly lay down beside her and stroked Charlene's waving arms and legs. 'You're like a little boxer,' she said, smiling. She counted her ten pinkies and played *This little piggy went to market*. It was boring; she was bored. Carly bounced up onto her knees and tickled Charlene's tummy. 'Shall we play chuff chuff trains again, Charlene?'

Charlene blinked, kicking her legs and gurgling.

Carly reached for her bedside cabinet. She pulled out her cigarettes and lighter and lit up, breathing in deeply. She knelt over Charlene and blew a thick plume of smoke directly into her face. 'Chuff chuff goes the steam engine.' She did it again and again as Charlene coughed and squirmed. Carly puffed smoke onto her baby until she'd finished the cigarette. Charlene whimpered and spluttered, crying.

Carly opened her bedroom window before dialling on her mobile. She crossed her legs, watching herself in the mirror. She felt quite grown up. 'Yes, I need another appointment with Dr Simon' – she glanced at Charlene, her little chest labouring up and down in wet grunts – 'as soon as possible, please.'

the good shepherd

Most of the students had gone home the week before. A skeleton staff kept the library open, mainly for the overseas postgraduate students, who studiously came to the library until it shut on Christmas Eve.

Carlos wondered what they did on Christmas Day when the library was shut. They were waiting at the library doors for it to open every day on the dot. He had no doubt their diligence would pay off; they would leave to become rich men and women.

'I'm from Chile,' he told Jean, the Scottish cleaner who never shut up.

'D'you ken what Christmas is all about?'

Carlos nodded. 'I am familiar with baby Jesus, the shepherds and the three wise men.' He turned to serve an Iranian student handing a book over. He caught her dark eyes in the peephole of her burkha. Carlos smiled. He didn't know if she smiled back. It seemed strange to him not to share the universal language of a smile. When he arrived in England thirty years ago, it was the only language he had. He wondered what non-Christian students thought of Christmas. He didn't think there would be many converts.

He liked the peace and quiet in the library after the frenzied run-up to the end of the first term. The new students were always giddy and immature. He spent large portions of the day wandering round hissing, 'Shh, this is a library.' As Christmas approached there'd be parties and more parties. Students laughed and giggled, arranging nights out. They texted and phoned each other noisily. Towards the end of term they walked round the library, burping, red-eyed. The toilets smelt of sick. Some of them didn't wash for days.

At twelve thirty, Carlos went into town for his lunch. The city centre Christmas lights flashed on and off. Christmas song medleys played again and again. He remembered as a child back home Christmas was like waiting for a real baby to be born. Then the baby arrived safely and everyone was glad. There was little fuss about presents.

Carlos was the security guard at the university library. He had no qualifications but had worked reliably at the library for so long he didn't need any. He knew the library inside out. He'd arrived in England as a young man, and the country had seemed very old and grey. It was a hard time for him, but he liked the royal family and their sense of duty. He tried to be like them, to have a bit of dignity. When students treated him like a second-class citizen, he'd go home and look at his photograph of the Queen above the fireplace and he'd remember – even if they had no manners, he did.

Over the years, colour had ceased to matter like it used to. Carlos knew that the hotchpotch of skin that streamed through the library doors was educated. He knew he was educated too, but without the bits of paper to prove it. He'd taught himself to read. Slowly at first, but he got faster. Carlos had read hundreds of books in the library, but still had no qualifications. It left a gnawing hunger inside him. He knew he'd have it for the rest of his life, like an ulcer, burning a hole in his heart.

Most of the students seemed to take their privileged life for granted. Carlos had overcome his bitterness; like the Queen in her *annus horribilis*, he believed one simply had to make the best of difficult situations.

Jean went to Scotland for Christmas and 'Hogmanay', as she called it. She'd stay with her daughter until the second of January. 'I cannae stay any longer, they'll not let me have a tab in the house and it's dreich outside.' She laughed with a juicy cough.

Carlos liked the university holidays because he could wander up and down the aisles and read what he liked, without being interrupted by gormless students who still didn't know how to borrow books.

Most of the students went home as soon as the term ended. The ones that stayed until Christmas Eve were anxious-looking – usually the ones that had re-sits as soon as they got back. Some of them, he knew, just didn't want to go home. There was a waif, a reed-like girl, whose shadow slipped over and under shelves. Her head wobbled on a bamboo stick neck, her blue hands fumbled to get her pass out of her bag. He'd read about eating disorders in one of the psychology books. He'd learnt to identify the students, usually girls, who had problems. She was the worst he'd seen. He didn't think she'd be eating turkey this Christmas – or anything.

Some of the students were in love and they couldn't bear to be apart over the Christmas break. They'd schmaltz in corridors, clinging to each other in passionate clinches behind books. Carlos imagined at their respective homes on Christmas Day they'd spend the whole day texting each other.

There were odd ones too, who'd have spent all term alone – and would stay on alone until the last minute. The boy in the baggy jumper was one of these. He'd been a problem for Carlos all term. He was noisy, in an unpredictable laddish way. He pestered girls who were never interested in him, and he tried too hard to impress the other boys by making a fool of himself. Carlos was no fashion expert, but he knew the ginger-haired, gangly, red-faced boy simply wasn't fitting in. He'd got very drunk at the end of term. Carlos was pretty sure it was his vomit he had to spray off the library wall. It was pink; he must've had a lot of red wine. In the week before

Christmas he'd seen him drunk outside the library a lot of times. He'd reel and shout as if a war had ended, or was beginning. Carlos had gone out one lunchtime. 'Please keep the noise down, you're disturbing students still trying to work.'

The boy had thrown his head back laughing. He'd pointed at Carlos, trying to get other students to join in jibing him. They'd turned their backs on him, muttering, 'Loser,' and walked away.

Carlos was a placid man, but he'd felt a rush of heat. 'I shall have to ask you to leave this area if you can't be quiet.'

Carlos could see the boy was under the influence of alcohol; he swayed, his arms and legs moving unreliably. Carlos had opened his mouth to tell him to move on, but stopped when the boy's eyes filled with tears. The boy spun, blankly staring at other students who sneered as they passed. Carlos watched the boy turn and run, his shirt tails flapping. His awkward limbs seemed way too big for his skinny frame – a little boy in a man's body.

The majority of kids left on December 19th. The baggy jumper boy had come every day since then. He'd be there at opening times, shivering without a coat, and he'd stay until closing time. When Carlos passed the desk the boy was supposedly working at, he had his head down and was snoring.

On December 21st, 22nd and 23rd, the boy avoided looking at Carlos as he opened up the library and studiously looked down at his shoes. On Christmas Eve, the library was closing at 4pm until December 27th. The boy had dark shadows hanging low beneath pooled eyes. It took Carlos a while to open up. His fingers were cold. The boy stood close, he smelt fusty.

Carlos let him in. The boy's nose was runny; he wiped it on his sleeve. He didn't have a bag with him for his studies. Carlos frowned. 'You're working hard.'

'Yeah,' the boy said, rubbing his hands together, 'I've got re-sits as soon as I get back.'

'Are you going home for Christmas?'

'Oh, yeah, yeah.' The boy sniffed. 'How about you?'

Carlos shook his head. 'Too far for me. I go to my neighbours', they are good people.'

The boy nodded, awkwardly shifting his weight from one foot to the other. 'That's good.'

'The peace and quiet in the library must be conducive to learning.'

'Yeah, suppose so.'

A couple of postgraduates came to the desk to ask for the opening hours. The boy slipped away.

Carlos planned to wander down to the cathedral and go to mass at 6pm. He liked the candles flickering, the carol singing and warmth of bodies next to him. The nativity manger and candles reminded him of home.

At three thirty, Carlos did a final lap of the library before locking up. He switched off a few computers that had been left on, and told an old, retired professor who was often in that he'd be shutting up soon.

'Thank you and happy Christmas,' the retired professor croaked. He always wore a dicky bow. His neck was so thin, it made Carlos think of a turkey, clucking before its cull.

The overseas students left in twos and threes. They'd spend Christmas together. Carlos wondered whether they pulled crackers or if it was just another day to them. Carlos read once about the First World War. The two enemies stopped fighting on Christmas Day and had a drink together. The image of them sitting together in peace made him feel better about his fellow man.

Carlos shut doors and switched off lights. It was the smell that drew him to the study room – a familiar, unwashed smell. Under a desk, he saw something sticking out. He bent down; it was a dirty old blanket. Carlos stood and rubbed his chin. He switched the light off but didn't lock the door. He came out and saw a shadow dart between shelves. He walked quickly to the aisle, but there was no one, only the smell of unwashed clothes lingering.

Carlos sighed heavily and looked up to heaven. He didn't want to make things worse for the boy with no friends. Every year at least one student attempted suicide; sometimes they succeeded. Carlos struggled to imagine the depths of misery those young people suffered – to have the world at their feet, and to choose to step off the edge. He cleared his throat and said, 'I'm going to lock up now.' He spoke loudly, adding, 'The third floor is the only floor that won't be alarmed.' Carlos left the library, locked the door, and went to mass.

Several times during the service, he broke out into a cold sweat. He was risking his job for a stupid, irresponsible student. He'd be sacked for incompetence if the library was broken into. It wasn't what the Queen would do – she always stuck to the rules. He bit his lip and prayed, *Please don't let the library be vandalised*. What if the boy went crazy? Images of books torn and ripped flashed in his head. He imagined the worst.

He slept very little and got up early on Christmas morning. He walked briskly. It was as if everyone had left the planet. The streets were completely deserted, not a soul about – except one.

He turned the lock of the library door and crept up to the third floor. Carlos had left the dim stairwell light on the day before, in case the boy was afraid of the dark.

Carlos peered in. The boy was curled up under the table, like a baby. Carlos pulled up a chair and watched over him until the boy sleepily opened his eyes. He blinked his eyes, focusing, and jerked upright like an animal caught in headlights.

Carlos held up his hand. 'Shh, it's alright. Come on, you can spend Christmas with me. I won't tell anyone.'

The boy's eyes filled with tears, he wiped his nose on his sleeve. 'I have nowhere to go…'

'Now you do. We shall make the best of it. We can watch the Queen's speech together.'

The boy nodded, sniffing. 'Yes, I like the Queen.'

cathy

You sip your coffee and type, *I've got to go now. Take care, be good, and I love you.* You go to the kitchen, fill the watering can and begin on the plants. Missy, the cat, tries to wrap herself around your legs. 'Are you missing him, too?' You pick her up and muzzle your face in her fur. 'It's not like he's completely away from us. With photos on Facebook, it's easy – we can see him every day, but no washing or cleaning up, no more grunts from him slumped in front of the TV. No more broken nights wondering, *When will he be back?* and *Will he remember to lock the door?*'

Missy purrs and jumps, scampering out into the garden.

You watch her sidle past the swing. You smile, remembering Johnny clambering up on the seat and swinging high, giggling with his baby-toothed grin. You sigh and pick up the watering can.

You flick through the newspaper and see there's a Monet exhibition on at the National Art Gallery in London. You decide to go. You plan to go alone so you can take in the art without having to chat about the merits of each with whomever you might have dragged along. You'll meander round Covent Garden after the exhibition, maybe do a bit of opportunistic shopping; bargain-hunting where no one knows you.

You catch the train and sit in the quiet compartment. You close your eyes, rocking with the clickety-clack, smoothly slicing through the countryside. A couple of teenagers laugh and giggle. It annoys you: why are they in the quiet coach? You shake your head, irritated with yourself. They're young, that's what it's all about – having fun. You move to a different part of the coach away from them. Happiness unsettles you.

At the exhibition you buy one of those audio guides, which explain each painting. You stop and listen to the soporific voice, allowing it to lull you. You let the details wash over you and people-watch. You wonder what they do in their lives, and where they are from, where they are going. You notice Italian and French women always seem very chic, their men handsome in rugged ways. They give each other opinions on the paintings. You and Paul would never do that sort of thing, he'd get bored and you'd feel awkward, knowing he was thinking you were trying to be clever. You think about what attracts couples to each other; once the kids have gone, what's left?

You catch a tour bus to see the London sights. The driver chats in an exaggerated cockney accent and points out various tourist highlights. You've been to London lots of times before, but this is an easy way to refresh your memory without getting sore feet. You think of when you'd brought Johnny for the first time and all he wanted to see was the Tower of London and the dungeons. You wonder why boys like the macabre and violent – all those ridiculous video games he played for hours.

The bus goes full circuit. It begins to all look the same. You watch drops of condensation form. They swell like tears, cutting a trail down the window. An elderly man sits next to you with a boy about five who jiggles a lot. The man wants to be friendly. He talks about the weather; it's easy – all you have to do is nod. Then he asks about your family. You tell him about Johnny being in Thailand.

'Oh gosh, does he like it there? Very different culture, isn't it?'

'Yes, he wanted something different. He dropped out of university – he didn't like the course. The trouble is they have to make a decision so young as to what they're going to do for the rest of their lives.'

'That's boys, it takes them longer to mature.' He ruffles the small boy's hair and asks, 'Why did he choose Thailand?'

'Lots of sunshine, lots of social life, lots of cheap drinks. Nothing altruistic, I'm afraid.'

'Kids nowadays,' the man laughs, 'they don't know they're born.'

You get off at Trafalgar Square for no other reason than you don't want to talk to him anymore. You watch the bus pull away and see the child waving until it goes around the corner. You don't wave back, you hate goodbyes. You walk and pass a man with a purple, blotchy face rummaging in a bin. You feel sorry for him. You wonder what he was in his life before, and where it all went wrong.

You window-shop and browse rails. You ask, 'How much is this dress?' knowing you'll never buy it. A young assistant thinks pink is your colour, but you prefer blue. The girl stifles a yawn. You thank her and tell her you'll think about which to choose. You walk the bustling pavements. People are texting or talking on their phones, all like Johnny – incapable of surviving without mobiles.

You pass a very posh-looking brasserie and decide to treat yourself for once, instead of grabbing a sandwich. The restaurant is supposedly French. The waiters teeter down a tightrope of good service on one side, and rude disregard for their patrons on the other. It's all quick flicks, and chins in the air. You smile at their antics. Johnny had said he was working in a restaurant. You can't imagine your lazy boy being much good, but maybe you're wrong. You hope so.

You order crab cakes with a salad. The food arrives with a theatrical flurry of shaken white serviettes. The meal looks pretty, an elegant piece of art. It seems a shame to spoil it by eating. It tastes delicious. You make yourself eat slowly. The portions are small; you know Paul would complain. You take your time, cut up your meal into parcels, aware of your manners. You watch couples who you guess are having affairs. For the lovers, the meal is a ploy of affection. Food is pushed around plates while hands entwine and feet play footsie. Mouthfuls are swallowed in suggestive ways. Food is licked and sucked, slowly, carefully. Married couples bicker and stab at their food, eat quickly and look out the window often. For the city business people, it's simply to gain nourishment; someone else is paying. Bite, chew and swallow.

You like to imagine they wonder what you do. You've made an effort with your clothes – dressed up for the trip. You hope they see more than a housewife with too much time on her hands. You wonder if the man on the bus will tell his wife about you when he gets home. He'll perhaps say, 'I met a woman on the bus. We chatted. No, I can't remember what she looks like.'

You eke the meal out with another coffee. You leaf though the book you bought at the exhibition, but don't concentrate on the pages, flicking and flicking, your eyes unfocused. Here it comes again – another wave. You despise your life. Since Johnny's left, the rest of your life looms ahead. You can't see beyond the huge crevice for you to fall down. Down and down. You make yourself not cry, you've got good at that. A gulp, a swallow, a small shake of the head. You reset your facial features as if in stone. You stare out the window. It starts raining heavily. People rush by like city rats scurrying for the nearest hole to shelter in.

The familiar figure hurries past in a rainy blur like everyone else. Head down, his hoodie pulled low against the pelting rain. Your heart skips. Johnny? It's him. You'd know your son anywhere. You saw that gangling gait, his Roman nose, his dark eyes. You stumble and make to run out after him but bump into a waiter. He steps back. 'Would you like your bill, madam?'

'I need to chase someone… my son… he's in Thailand… but I saw…'

'I'll bring it to you swiftly then, madam,' he says stiffly.

You try to dodge round him. 'I'll come back for it, honestly I will. Ten minutes at the most. I must hurry.'

'It would be better to pay now.' He moves slightly, blocking you.

Customers look up from their tables. He won't move aside.

'Of course, of course.' You rush back to the table where you left your bag, and scoop up your purse, fumbling for some cash. 'Damn, I'll have to pay with my card.'

'Not a problem, madam. Please follow me.'

'Please hurry.' Your fingers tremble as you punch in your bank card number, your eyes dart across to the window again and again.

You snatch the card out as soon as it's processed. You leave the waiter waving your receipt. You pull your coat on while running. You realise as soon as you step out you've left your umbrella in the restaurant, with the Monet book. It doesn't matter. Nothing matters except catching up with him.

Your mind cartwheels: if he's in Thailand, why is he here in London? He was meant to be there. Maybe none of it is true? Could it be possible? The emails and photos... they could be from anywhere? Taken any time? Your heart pounds, it *is* possible. You push and shove through the crowds. You weave in and out, catching elbows and arms. You gasp when you see his long-legged lope in the distance. He's across the road. You shout, 'Johnny, Johnny!'

People turn to the woman waving with both arms – but he doesn't. He'll have his ear thingies in, you think. He's always listening to music. You ignore the red pedestrian crossing and dodge in and out of cars. Fists are shaken, horns beep; one car makes an emergency stop, another veers. You are oblivious to it all.

You get to the other side of the road, keep running, hands out, fingertips stretched to reach and pull your son's arm.

The boy spins round. 'What the hell...?'

You clutch his arm tight, unable to breathe properly. You stare at his face, lift your hand to touch him. A young boy so like your Johnny.

'What?' he says again, stepping back.

You drop your hands, let them hang at your sides. 'I'm sorry, I thought you were someone else...'

He frowns and walks quickly. He doesn't look back.

You stare until he disappears.

The wave comes again. You close your eyes, clench your fists, fighting the urge to scream.

You hear a school bell, it's home time. Children pour out of the school gates, screeching and yelling, happy to be free. They stampede past you. You look at their feet, their clattering shoes. You remember tying Johnny's shoelaces, teaching him a life skill: under, over, round and through. He was a quick learner. You notice very few children wear laces nowadays. It's all Velcro and slip-ons, or trainers.

You take a big breath and set off to get the train back home. Your feet are tired and aching after all the running. You bend to loosen the brown brogues you have on. They were Johnny's. They're far too big for you, but tied tightly and with two pairs of socks on, they do. Somehow, wearing them makes you feel closer to him. You swing one foot in front of the other, touch the ground, and again – one in front of the other, left then right and back to the ground.

This time, the wave comes faster. It's upon you before you can run. It sweeps you off your feet. You stumble and fall to your knees. You stay on all fours, hitting the ground again and again with your fists until your knuckles bleed. You shake your head and howl as if rabid. You claw at your feet, scrabbling to pull the shoes off. You frighten people. They stand and watch but daren't touch you. They wonder who you are.

You always are, and always will be, the woman whose son went travelling and hung himself with his shoelaces.

being normal

I've always liked going to disabled toilets; it's just something I like to do, a bit of a treat. They're bigger with extra knobs and buzzers. The lighting and whole ambience is kinder, there's a softness added to the rigmarole of ablutions. I admire the superior standard of workmanship that you don't see in regular public conveniences. The flush mechanisms are always a delight: some are push buttons, some flush when you stand up, some when you put the seat down. There's a wide variety of taps, too: some you twist, others you pull, some you wave near them, others you simply stroke. It's like an interactive quiz, I give myself marks out of ten. Everything is easy to use: big handles for arthritic hands, large signs for the partially blind, a set of white monkey bars for the legless, and buzzers here, there, and everywhere for emergency moments. I'd love to press or pull one of them, to try it out with '*Please would you pass me the toilet paper?*' That sort of behaviour could get me banned for life – it's not worth the risk. Instead I stoke the cords and switches gently.

There's a frisson in going to a disabled toilet when you're not disabled. People are very righteous about it, care needs to be taken. Often the disabled toilets are set away from the main run of cubicles, as if removed to a higher place of dignity. These are a doddle to slip into and click the door shut unnoticed. I like to linger. It's so white and shiny and clean. The soap dispenser is usually full, and smells nice, instead of disinfectant. I run my hands along the squeaky clean tiles, touch the soft toilet paper, wipe my nose with the velvety hand towels and sit and ponder. It's a little oasis of peace, like a prayer room.

Occasionally someone has knocked on the door. 'Are you alright in there?'

'Oh yes,' I say in my well-practised frail voice, 'I'll be out as soon as I can.' They usually leave, but if they persist in hovering outside, I give them an over-share: 'I get terribly constipated nowadays. It's my bowels, like hard gun pellets and...'

Twice, I've been caught out. I was coming out of the toilet and someone in a wheelchair was waiting. The first time, I was quick-thinking and incorporated a swinging limp and goofy grin. The lady in the wheelchair gave me a sweet smile of solidarity, a fellow comrade fighting against the odds.

The second time, I was met almost nose-to-nose by a red-faced carer ramming her charge into me. 'What you doing using the disabled, eh? She's just about wet herself.'

I was aware of women glancing over their shoulders as they did their lipstick. Some stopped and turned, frowning.

I did the only thing I could do – I stared through her. 'Who said that?' I asked, looking around blankly.

'Don't give me that,' the Rottweiler barked. 'You saw me clear enough when you opened the door. Gave you a start, didn't I?'

'I'm s-s-s-sorry,' I stuttered, and even though I say it myself, I do a splendid stutter. 'I'm, I'm...' – a little crowd was gathering – 'I've lost my white stick. I th-th-thought it would be okay to use this WC...'

A bony woman, who probably spent her youth on Greenham Common, came to my rescue. She shook her long, straggly hair and rattled her be-jangled arms. 'You can't victimise her – she's disabled, too. Disability isn't a competition. She deserves equal rights.'

'Mind your own business,' the unpleasant woman sneered, and

with that she barged the wheelchair past me into the toilet. I obligingly tottered sideways so several of the onlookers rushed forward to steady me as she slammed the door. There was much 'No need for that' and 'What a disgraceful attitude', and so on. The righteous and the just were high on their horses. I blusteringly thanked them, and did some spectacular gurning. It did the trick and frightened away all further offers of assistance. I wobbled off, blinking, leaving them to discuss the finer details of political correctness.

Six months later, I'd more or less forgotten the incident and was enjoying a spot of shoplifting. A similar pleasure to using disabled toilets – in its thrill of possibly getting caught. I'd popped a very red, shiny, tarty number in my bag. I'd never wear it, of course, but it screamed *take me* with such urgency, I had to have it. I was on my way out when who should I bump into but Rotty the Rottweiler.

She snarled, 'I remember you.'

It took me a moment or two, which was to my advantage. 'Who are you?' I asked innocently.

'You know bloody well who I am. I was nearly lynched when I came out of the toilet after your little sob story. Not so blind now, are you? I saw you come up and down that escalator no problem.'

'Yes, I can see now, but I couldn't then – the doctors have cured me. Now excuse me.'

'Not so fast.' She grabbed my arm and hissed, 'If I ever catch you playing that trick again' – she nipped hard – 'you'll be sorry.'

She annoyed me intensely so I let rip. 'Help, she's crazy!' I screamed like a banshee. 'She's attacking me. Help!' I kicked her hard on the shin. The burly security men barrelled to my rescue and yanked her away from me. I cowered under the shower of rude obscenities she yelled over her shoulder as they hauled her out.

The department store manager, appreciating the trauma I'd undergone, insisted I had a cup of sweet tea before leaving: 'Good for shock, my dear.'

I sipped the tea with a small smile, wondering where she was now. For good measure, I'd slipped the red dress into her bag, amidst the melee. The security alarm had bleeped furiously as she was ejected.

Months have passed since then and remembering the incident never fails to make me titter. I've considered notching up the disability lark with a wheelchair, but they cost a fortune – even for three-wheeled ones on ebay. I've tentatively looked into getting one on the NHS, but you have to have all sorts of tests and assessments. Instead, I settle for a spot of shoplifting; it always cheers me up.

It's at the precinct I see her. She's pushing the wheelchair. I watch her from the upper floor as she ploughs into crowds without so much as a by your leave. She's like a gladiator tearing through. There's an arrogant anger about her that irritates me, as if the world owes her. I watch her hurling snarls left and right, tutting and sighing, shoving and pushing. She catches ankles and toes as she charges along. I shake my head. I know if I was responsible for a wheelchair, it would be a pleasant sojourn. We would chat happily, perhaps laughing as we went; people would smile, I would return their smiles bashfully and they'd comment on my caring ways.

Rotty pushes the wheelchair to the lift and jabs the button. I head for WH Smith, which is next to the lift doors. I wait, and peep out from behind a magazine. They roll out of the lift and stop near the food hall at the top of the escalator. Rotty leans over her charge and says something. She points to a café, and the woman nods. Rotty puts the wheelchair brakes on, and goes into the café alone – I suppose to see if there's a table free.

It is my only chance. I hurry out, slip behind the wheelchair, and undo the brake. I give the wheelchair the daintiest of pushes – it's a careless accident waiting to happen.

I fly down the stairs, hot on the heels of Rotty, who is hysterically screaming. She throws herself prostrate on the floor, next to the carnage. A crowd gathers around the bloody heap at the bottom of the stairs. Everyone is pushing and shoving and elbowing each other aside for a nosy.

The spectators are stunned and an ambulance is called for. Rotty wails uncontrollably and clutches the flaccid body. There is an uncertain hush. I whisper to no one in particular, 'She left the brakes off. Some people aren't safe to be out with a wheelchair.'

A couple of eyebrows raise, a few heads shake, elbows nudge, mouths turn down. The crowd are soon casting mental stones. The police and ambulance arrive – both appealing for witnesses.

'She left the wheelchair at the top of the escalator with the brakes off,' says a middle-aged woman, pointing an accusing finger at Rotty.

'Tragic, an avoidable accident,' says a tweedy man with a cravat.

'Shameful,' mutters a young mother with a pushchair.

Rotty looks around the gathered circle. Maybe she sees me, maybe not – she has a strange, blank-eyed stare.

'There's something not right with her,' a voice murmurs.

'She's not all there,' another says, nodding.

I smile wisely. I already know – people can look normal, but often they're not.

one in a thousand

Baby Maeve was born on September 17th, 1989; a normal delivery weighing in at seven pounds and ten ounces. They'd got a shortlist of names, but when she arrived with her milky skin and shock of black hair, she was Maeve.

Mike wept holding Maeve in his arms. He shook his head. 'You were brilliant, Karen, brilliant. Look at her, our daughter, she's gorgeous.'

Karen pulled the baby blanket down and peered into the bundle. The black hair reminded her of a cat. Baby purred, her eyes flickering open – they were foggy grey. Karen flopped back on the hospital sheets exhausted and watched Mike tenderly holding their baby. He couldn't look away, as if he was bewitched.

It was the middle of the night when she was taken up to the ward. The nurses seemed pleased with her; she'd been uncomplicated, a normal delivery with no fuss. She heard the nurses rushing back and forward, flicking lights on and off, gossiping about a birth on the delivery suite that afternoon. 'Like an octopus,' she heard a nurse whisper. 'A freak,' the porter shuddered. Karen drifted off to sleep, with strange dreams whirling.

She was woken by a mewling sound from the cot. The nurse switched her night light on. 'You need to feed your baby, she's crying.'

Karen got out of bed, surprised she could stand, that life went on. She peered into the cot, waiting for a surge of love – to be awash with maternal longing – but all she saw and felt was a baby crying and everyone expecting her to make it stop. The tiny white and black thing clenched its fists. She was unsure which bit to pick up. The nurse said kindly, 'Why don't you sit down and I'll pass her to you.'

Karen sat, and the nurse laid the ball of hunger near her swollen, engorged breasts. 'You need to put her to your nipple.'

Karen had opted for breastfeeding – she dared not. *Breast is best* had been drummed into them all at the NCT classes. Wicked and weak was the woman who relied on bottles. Karen uncertainly undid her nightie, the baby pummelled at her skin. She limply held the heap of fury. The nurse gently pushed the black head into her nipple. Karen felt pincers of pain. The nurse held the head in place and Maeve got the hang of sucking.

'Is it meant to hurt so much?' Karen asked.

'It'll get easier once your nipples harden,' smiled the nurse. 'You'll get the hang of it. Best for baby and best for you.'

Never, thought Karen.

At visiting time, Karen obligingly smiled, took the flowers and munched the grapes. Mike was besotted, he baby-talked into Maeve's face, cooing. After thirty minutes, Karen touched his arm. 'I'm really tired, do you mind if I take a nap?'

'Oh God, of course, darling. I'm sorry, so thoughtless. I'll leave my girls to get a rest.'

He tenderly placed Maeve back in her cot and bent to kiss Karen. He'd done the same twenty-four hours ago before they'd driven to the hospital. He'd held her between contractions and kissed her saying, 'Tomorrow, we'll be a family.' She'd nodded – she thought it was what she wanted.

As he kissed her forehead, Karen asked, 'Aren't you going to take her with you for a little while?'

Mike looked puzzled. 'No, darling, she needs to stay with you for her feeds.'

'Oh.'

Karen couldn't sleep; she was buzzing, wide awake. She listened to the ward clatter: the nurses chatting, babies crying, mothers murmuring. Baby Maeve in the cot next to her bed grumbled then howled. Karen stayed still. An older Irish nurse came to see why she wasn't feeding her. 'I've tried,' Karen lied. 'I don't think I've enough milk.'

'Well, let's give her a bottle to tide her over and you can try again tomorrow. Sometimes it takes a while for your milk to come through properly.'

Karen asked, 'Could you give her this bottle? My belly is really sore.'

The nurse sat next to Karen and gave Maeve the bottle. 'What a lovely name for a lovely baby,' she cooed.

Karen felt overwhelming relief as the baby guzzled the bottle, slurping and gulping, away from her. Once fed, Maeve relaxed her fists, her crumpled face ironed out smooth again. The nurse gently laid her back in the cot and she slept.

It only lasted three hours, then the whimpers grew to growls; hunger leapt out, running through the shadows. It filled corners, rattled windows, pulled curtains. Karen bit her fingernails. How could something so little be so big? The ward clattered and clanged, everything loud and bright; it smelt of sweaty women and birth. Karen wanted to be home – a home before all this, before *it* came and started crying.

The Irish nurse was by her bed again. Karen had put her fingers in her ears, her eyes closed.

She touched Karen's elbow. 'Wouldn't you have a little go yerself?'

Karen bit her lip. 'I can't, not tonight. Just help me out tonight. Please.'

Nurse Riley looked at Karen's face and her wide eyes, pleading. She sighed and turned to the cot to sort out baby Maeve.

Karen sheepishly asked the nurse, 'Do you think she smells funny?'

'Your baby? She smells divine, a gorgeous baby smell.'

Karen nodded and wrinkled her nose. 'Oh.'

The breastfeeding nurse specialist came to Karen the next morning. She was a big woman with a shelf bosom. 'The night staff said you had trouble feeding last night. Shall we try again? ' She talked with her head on one side and smelt of pear drops and baby sick.

Karen wanted to hit her. There was no *we,* this was all up to her.

She watched the nurse lift Maeve out of the cot and hand her over. Maeve nuzzled in Karen's nightie. Karen glanced at her, *a parasite.* 'I'm sorry,' Karen pleaded, 'can you give her a bottle this feed? I'm too tired.'

The nurse pursed her lips. 'I don't think you've tried very hard.'

'I have,' flared Karen.

The nurse raised an eyebrow and took a frantic Maeve off Karen. 'Mummy's tired. We'll give you a bottle this time, baby, but next feed, we'll try again, eh?' She looked at Karen, waiting.

Karen nodded weakly, too relieved to feel guilty.

Karen didn't go to the dayroom to talk to the other mums. She didn't want to swap birth details or baby talk. She stayed by her bed, pretending to read. The auxiliaries came to make up fresh beds. She heard them talk about the baby in room two: 'It has a syndrome. It has to go for surgery this morning.'

Karen wished her baby was going for surgery, that it could be wheeled away, that it wasn't next to her all the time, sniffling and scuffling.

She remembered a story in the papers years ago about a baby stolen from a hospital ward; it was never found. Karen thought about the story a lot.

Mike visited in the afternoon. Karen told him, 'My milk still hasn't come through.' He happily gave Maeve her bottle, all gooey-eyed, crooning as she slurped. Karen winced at the happy scene. It stirred something deep inside her: disgust.

In the middle of the night, Maeve was a bundle of bawling hunger again. Karen stayed rigid in bed, frozen in fear. Nurse Riley eventually came to her and gently lifted Maeve out of the cot, handing her to Karen.

'She won't feed, I've tried,' blurted Karen. She had no intention of putting Maeve near her breast again. Her skin prickled, she pulled her nightie tighter together.

Nurse Riley cooed, 'Let's give her a bottle, eh?' She crooned and cuddled the burning baby, eventually calming Maeve enough to take the milk. She sat opposite Karen. 'You must be tired, eh?'

'I can't get the hang of breastfeeding.'

'Don't worry, pet, it's not for everyone despite what the NCT say. Nutty Condescending Toffs, that's what we say it stands for in the trade.'

Karen gave a small smile.

'You've got a beautiful baby here.' She put Maeve back in the cot. 'Night night, beauty.'

'Do you think she has a syndrome?' Karen asked.

'No, she's perfect. What on earth makes you say that?'

'She makes strange noises and smells… not good.'

Nurse Riley laughed. 'You really are a new mum. You'll get used to it all.'

Karen drifted off. She woke with a start, her heart hammering; she could hardly breathe. When the panic passed, she stayed awake, staring into darkness, too afraid to dream.

Day three, Karen was due to go home. She dressed with a dry throat, her mouth full of sawdust. A nurse with butterfly eyes took Maeve away for a heel prick or something. She brought her back and offered her to Karen.

'Put *it* back in the cot,' Karen barked.

The nurse looked confused. She took Maeve away again and must have changed and fed her. She was quiet. Karen felt numb, as if the epidural had spread through her whole body. She stared into space.

When Mike arrived on the ward with the carrycot they'd chosen together, the sister in charge touched his arm and asked him to come to the office for a chat.

Karen stared blankly. Everything was beginning to make sense – the room she'd given birth in was room number six. Karen cracked her fingers, clicked her teeth, walked in circles. She threaded words together, ready to explain, to tell Mike what was happening, but when he arrived they slipped away, her sentences unravelling.

Mike sat next to Karen's bed with a fixed smile. 'Hey darling, how are you doing?'

He bent to kiss her. Her head felt too heavy to lift off the pillow, *it* was sucking the life out of her. Her mouth opened and closed in billowing, white, absent spaces – words evaporated. She watched him stare at the cot, immediately he was under *its* spell. She was the only one who knew what was happening. She had to fight *its* evil alone. She fought back tears.

Mike rubbed his forehead. 'Erm, sweetheart, the nurses think it might be better if you stayed another night.'

Karen clung to the notion in desperation. 'Yes, that's a good idea.' She wanted to be alone so she could think about what she could do. Mike couldn't see the evil – none of them could. It was all going to be up to her.

He looked sad. 'Don't you want to hold her?' he asked.

He didn't understand, that's how *it* worked, leaking evil through *its* skin when held, that's why he was besotted.

Mike gave Maeve a bottle when it was clear Karen wasn't going to move as the bawling and whirling fists got worse. Karen dared to glance quickly as he fed her, she didn't want to risk any of *its* powerful rays. She saw *it* gathering strength, getting nourishment, everyone was falling for it; *it* was too clever for them all. Mike held *it* to his chest to burp, that was dangerous – heart to heart was *its* most powerful position.

She said cheerily, 'She'll be fine now, put her back for a sleep.'

'I'll just give her a little cuddle.'

'Put *it* back now!' Karen shouted.

He gently placed Maeve in her cot and covered her in a blanket, worriedly glancing at Karen. Once settled, he brought his chair up close. 'Honey, the nurses think that maybe tomorrow you should see a doctor to chat over things.'

'What things?'

'How you feel about the baby and stuff. Don't you love our baby?'

Oh dear. He was absolutely in *its* control; she needed to tread carefully. *It* snuffled as if to warn her of *its* power. Karen smiled with effort. 'Of course I'll see the doctor.' She squeezed his hand and kept her lips sealed.

He kissed Maeve first and then Karen. 'See you tomorrow, sweetie.'

As soon as he left, she wiped her face where he'd kissed, in case any of *its* power had been transferred.

That night, Nurse Riley lifted a starved, wailing Maeve. 'Come on, Karen, shall we try and feed her together, eh?' She spoke to her as if she was subnormal.

Karen felt *it* gather strength, eyes glowing red, the smell stronger, *its* voice deep and devilish. She lay absolutely still, staring at the ceiling, deaf and dumb until Nurse Riley gave up trying to talk to her and took *it* away for another feed. Karen knew she would look at *its* eyes and be bewitched. They were all under *its* spell.

It was a full moon. Karen knew that was a good sign. She remembered the story about the missing baby. She had to be quick, into the nursery and out, skidding up the hospital corridors, jumping the cracks – that'd be bad luck.

At 3am, the ward sister met a dishevelled Mike hurrying up the corridor. Her eyes were red, as if she'd been crying. She touched his elbow gently and led him into the 'quiet room'.

A sad-looking doctor was waiting for him. He stood. 'Hi, Mike. Take a seat, please.'

The office smelt of BO. There were plastic flowers on a filing cabinet, and a half-eaten box of chocolates with a thank-you card on the table between them. The doctor pushed them aside with a sigh. He shifted in his chair, it squeaked. The sister came back with a tray of sweet tea, and left again.

The doctor leant forward, holding his hands loosely together between his knees. 'I'm afraid we have bad news...'

the suitcase

Jim checked himself in the hall mirror before setting out for the train. He was neatly shaved, his hair combed meticulously to the left, shirt sharply ironed, tie knotted centrally. He'd buffed his shoes the night before. He felt jittery and hadn't been able to eat breakfast. He managed half a cup of coffee with small sips and swallows.

Donna was surprised he had to go to London. 'What, to teach you to put library books back on shelves properly?'

'Probably new technology or something,' he mumbled. He hated lying to her. They were childhood sweethearts and had lived in Seal Bay all their lives. It was a genteel kind of place, peculiarity didn't go down well.

He waved *'bye* and shut their cottage front door. It was a beautiful summer's day, the birds were singing. Across fields, he could see the sea dissolving into a blue sky. He waved to Michael Main, the local bobby, on the other side of the cricket field. They'd been in the same class at school. It was that kind of place.

London – the big smoke, where it *could* be a different world. He checked and double-checked his suitcase lock. He'd bought the case especially for the trip. It was inconspicuous brown leather, with a very good lock. He'd packed precisely, everything was organised in polythene bags. He sat where he could see the suitcase on the train, and kept an eye on it.

A Slavic girl checked him in at the B&B. It was small and discreet. He paid in cash. She handed his room key over, saying, 'Continental breakfast outside your room at 8am.'

Jim nodded. 'Thank you.' He didn't tell her he'd be long gone by then.

He found his room at the top of a winding staircase. He turned the key, it sounded very loud. He took in the decor of the room. It was more of a hostel, no pictures or ornaments, orange walls, and a small sink in the corner. He wondered whether the girl would remember him if anyone asked her to describe him.

He looked round for a mirror. He couldn't manage without a mirror. He opened the small, free-standing wardrobe; it creaked ajar. He wilted with relief, there was a mirror stuck on the inside door; it was slightly distorted, but he'd manage.

He put the suitcase on the bed and stroked the travelling dust off it. For years he'd wanted to do this. He took a big breath, got the key out, and opened it. The polythene bags lay folded neatly in layers. He lifted them, placing them on the bed one by one.

He'd decided weeks ago on his itinerary. He'd arrive in London at twelve, get to the B&B by one, and spend at least an hour getting ready. Then he'd go to the National Gallery. He'd spend a couple of hours there, and later find somewhere to eat. Maybe he'd go to a few bars after. He didn't want to be too rigid. For once in his life he'd try and go with the flow.

He opened the first bag slowly and lifted out the dress. He'd wrapped it in tissue paper because he loved the rustling sound. It was beautiful, made of silk, in a Japanese kimono style, blue and green hues. He hung it up and stroked the material; it felt luxurious. Next, he lifted the stockings out one by one. They floated, light as cobwebs, proper sheer stockings and suspenders, none of those pull-up tights. The lady in the lingerie shop had been very helpful. 'I'm sure your wife will love them.' She'd packaged them carefully with a pretty bow. Next, he lifted up the shoes; he adored shoes.

High stilettos, they were agony, but worth it. They matched the dress, and had the cutest little T-bar. Lastly, he took out the wig, a blonde bob. It framed his face perfectly.

He undressed and hung up his clothes. Then he watched himself as he shaved his legs in front of the mirror. After moisturising, he slid the stockings on, carefully drawing them over his calves and up to his thighs. They felt delicious, five-denier, the finest he could buy. 'Like a second skin,' the lady in the shop had smiled. He indulged himself and paraded around the room in his silk and satin underwear, swishing as he moved, looking at his reflection coyly over his shoulder. He sat in front of the mirror, crossed his legs and leant forward to apply his make-up. He brushed his eyelids, blending shadows to make his eyes look bigger. False eyelashes next, gluing them on carefully. He blinked twice to check they were comfortable. He dusted blusher on top of his foundation to accentuate his cheekbones. For several weeks on a Wednesday evening, while Donna was at her pilates class, he'd been practising with shades and colours to get the right balance. The autumn range seemed to be best suited to his skin. He put lipstick on, circling round, making sure none was on his teeth, and that his lips were glossy. Finally, he slipped the wig on. He patted his bob, turning one way then the other. He puckered his lips and blew himself a kiss. With a blast of perfume, he clicked his small, silver bag shut, and set off.

He had to walk slowly because of the shoes. He stepped out of the dark hallway into bright sunshine. He felt like a butterfly emerging from a cocoon. He noticed people glance at him. He felt liberated; the more they stared, the more confident he felt. Some school kids jeered and laughed. Jim patted his hair as he passed them. 'Good day, children.'

It sent them into fits of hysterics. He tittered himself.

At the National Gallery, he spent a long time appraising each picture. He liked standing elegantly, his bag swinging playfully from his arm. He looked at his ankles, which seemed sexily slender in his shoes. Two old women walked by; one nudged the other. 'I told you so,' she hissed, 'it's one of those transvestites.'

'They want to be women, don't they?'

He could've explained, but they wouldn't understand. It was the dressing-up he liked, that's all, the sensuous thrill of it. He knew Donna wouldn't understand either – he didn't understand, himself, but was driven to do it.

He nodded to them in a friendly manner. Tight-lipped, they tutted and scurried away.

Jim spent a long time in the Picasso exhibition trying to interpret the imagery. He couldn't pretend to understand its meaning, and yet the art fascinated him. He was vaguely aware of being stared at and enjoyed the attention. He made sure his posture was perfect. He felt he had a look of Kate Moss.

He turned to smile broadly at his admirer and almost fell off his heels with a start. Donna's sister, Tina, was staring; staring so hard it was rude. She flickered recognition. He turned and tottered as fast as his heels allowed. He hurried to the toilets, making the mistake of barging into the men's first, and running back out into the ladies. He dived into a cubicle and slammed the door. He slumped on the seat, head in his hands. He bit his knuckle. What was Tina doing here? No one who lived in Seal Bay should be here in London. She worked in the greengrocers, she should be at work, there was no reason she should ever visit London. Why wasn't she behind her till packing potatoes up for pensioners? He tried to stop the rising panic.

He breathed heavily until his galloping pulse calmed. She could be anywhere, but he couldn't hide in the toilet all day. He nervously re-applied his lipstick, round and round his lips, leaving no smudges.

He left the gallery by the back entrance, hurrying. He glanced repeatedly over his shoulder as he tottered along briskly. He soon got blisters. His stockings were ruined and he was limping. He looked down at his feet and thought how he'd have to get the

Underground back. His confidence was shattered. The stares and titters now seemed tauntingly cruel. He wanted to be anonymous, to be Mr boring Jim again – instantly forgettable.

He headed towards the Underground. People brushed against him. He held the handrail tight, unsteady on his heels. He kept close to the sweaty walls, his face down, shirking into the shadows.

The platform was heaving. Commuters packed in shoulder to shoulder. It was stiflingly hot. Jim's eyes prickled, he could feel his make-up running with sweat. His false eyelashes itched with the city's grit.

He clutched his bag tight. When he'd set out in his women's clothes he'd felt like a bird set free, flying high. Now he was clipped, a freak exhibit in a cage. He felt ugly, an untouchable leper. He looked up at the board, three minutes until the next tube arrived.

Someone tapped his shoulder.

He turned to face Tina.

She looked him up and down with a smirk. 'I followed you. I thought it was you in the gallery. Well, well, well' – she nodded her head – 'this certainly is a turn-up for the books.'

He reached out to her. 'Tina, you don't understand. It isn't what you think, I'm not...'

She glanced at his perfectly painted nails on her arm and interrupted him. 'Oh, I most certainly do understand. Poor Donna, I always thought you weren't right for her, you've always been shifty...'

'No, Tina, you've got this all wrong. Me and Donna, we're very happy. This is a one-off. I needed to get it out of my system, it's complicated...'

Tina's cheeks flushed. 'Get your filthy, perverted hand off my arm. It's not complicated, it's very simple: you're a lying, cheating–'

He clutched her sleeve. 'Please, at least let me try and explain. It's a fetish. I'm not cheating on Donna. It's simply an urge.'

'Let go,' she snapped, pulling away to shake him off.

He tightened his grip.

Her toxic words were drowned out by the whoosh of the Tube train arriving. The pushing crowd behind swelled forward. Jim's silky dress lifted like Marilyn Monroe's. The warm heat rushed. People blinked as the grimy, hot air blew and the brakes screeched in unison with a woman's high-pitched cry. The metallic, white noise melded with the screams that echoed down the dank tunnel walls.

When the emergency services arrived, too late for yet another Tube fatality, the police appealed for witnesses – a thankless task in the chaos.

The fading lights of the last London train to leave Seal Bay Station disappeared. Jim's brogues echoed on the empty platform. He loosened his tie, and undid his shirt top button, breathing deep gulps of Seal Bay's salty air.

Michael Main stepped out of the shadows. 'Hello, Jim. I'm afraid I'm here with bad news.' Michael held his hand out. 'Here, let me take your suitcase.'

survivor

'Be careful of Sergeant Burns, he's a got a screw loose.'

'What d'you mean?' said Private Dawson, who'd been called up for his first piece of action.

'He's different…' Private Stevens shrugged. 'He's not normal.'

'Have you been on patrols with him?'

'Yeah, and he's worse than the enemy – shoots first, thinks later. He doesn't care who the enemy is, as long as he's got an enemy. We went into one village and he ordered us to shoot on sight.' Private Stevens shook his head. 'I could hear kids crying. I told Burns and he shoved his nose in my face and said, "Question my orders again, soldier, and I'll shoot you." Christ, he meant it. I could see it in his eyes. He's mental.'

Zac hitched up his torn trousers, and lay on his belly on the path next to the curling mat of carpet and empty bottles. It was a hot August day, even the weeds were wilting. Zac found the magnifying glass down the back alley. It took him a while to work out what it did. He held the big, fat glass eye close to his watery blue pupil. Giant bees buzzed, four-foot caterpillars shuffled, blades of grass swished like glinting swords. It illuminated a city of ants, the black thread weaving forward and backwards, a mesmerising military column. He studied them and carefully aimed: *fizz, phfutt,* they popped in the heat. Angling his laser beam, he took them out, one by one, leaving singed full stops. They were stupid, they didn't run away. More and more came, he could do it all day. They kept coming forward, doing the suicide shuffle. He had to stop when it got dark. He thought about them later at night while his mam and her new boyfriend, Mick, screamed at each other.

From the top deck of the bus, he shot people with his fingers. 'Bam, bam – you're dead.'

Mark Wood showed him how to make a catapult. They started with the cat. Zac quickly moved on to the lower school, but had the catapult confiscated when he nearly took Jason Dunne's eye out.

He shook salt on slugs in the back yard; they turned inside out, leaving a snotty, messy trail. He wished it was Wayne, his half brother.

Zac lived in Blackpool. He loved the sea; in September, the waves were wild.

'It's to do with the moon,' Wayne told him. Wayne read science books.

The waves smashed against the wall. Every year, the white horses would rear up and kick someone over. They'd be dragged into the water, under and down. It was always front page in the *Evening Chronicle*. Zac loved the raging waves; he loved dicing with death.

Friday afternoon double science seemed to drag on forever. He watched the Bunsen burner flutter blue wings. He turned his flame into a spear of white anger. He stared at the teacher's red face while he yelled, 'I'm sick of you messing around, Zachary.'

Everyone knew not to call him Zachary. Zac fingered the rusty penknife in his pocket. *One day, you'll regret that, shitface.* At last, the bell went and he ran. He ran out of school, down the streets and onto the promenade leading down to the sea. He stripped off, took a deep breath and ran over sand dunes, across the rippling, hard, wrinkled sand and into the snapping waves. Knee deep, they knocked him down. He jumped up, leaping above them, willing them higher. He threw his head back. The sea made him crazy – he liked being mad. He could feel the current but he was a good swimmer, his arms and legs like flippers. He slipped underwater and shot up again. He wanted to feel the sea chuck him around, to fight and win.

After an hour he turned to the shore, surprised at how far away the beach was. The sun sunk lower, long red fingers stroked the horizon. He was getting tired and couldn't touch the seabed. He put his head down and began swimming, but those long red fingers pulled him back. The waves tossed him like a ball. He gulped air, cracking the surface, mouth gasping. He glimpsed figures on the beach, they were tiny dots. Every now and then a huge wave would crash over him. He'd cough, swimming to the surface, gagging. The sky was darkening, he was too tired to swim; he doggy paddled, scrambling in the churning waves.

Time dissolved into a bruised sky. He glimpsed grey tassels of the shore. He could make out shadowy figures and heard a dog barking. He couldn't shout – he didn't have the breath to spare. At last he felt a brush of seaweed, a few metres further forward and his toes touched the seabed. He propelled himself forward with small pushes on the sand. He jumped as waves came. If he timed it right, he could get forward before the ebb pulled him back.

He saw the next wave race towards him, looming high above. With the last breath of air screaming in his lungs he jumped and surfed on the crest, his heart fit to burst. He battled, arms and legs thrashing. The wave swept up to the shore and chucked him onto the beach – a piece of debris.

He dragged himself up and zigzagged unsteadily before flopping down onto the cold sand. The beach was lit under a full moon. He lay listening to the waves, his heart settling. He opened his eyes; he was alive. He pushed handfuls of sand close to his face, staring hard at the thousands of particles running through his fingers. *I nearly died. I'd be like one of those ants I popped, a black full stop.*

When he felt strong enough to stand, he felt strange – a survivor. He pulled his clothes on and shivered his way home.

'Where the hell have you been?' His mam pulled on her fag, tapping her foot. 'I've missed the bingo because of you. You were meant to be minding our Stacey.'

'Couldn't Wayne have minded Stacey?'

'Wayne couldn't mind a bleedin' hamster in a cage. He has enough bother minding himself.'

'Where's my tea?'

'You're joking? I'm not waiting on you hand and foot when you can't do me one little favour.' She ground her fag out and pulled on her coat. 'Get yerself some toast. I'll be back late.' She slammed the door.

'She's been a right cow since Mick left,' he muttered.

He spread marg across his toast and smeared it heavily with jam. He didn't mind Stacey, but it was a pain in the arse having to mind her. *Bloody Wayne, he's useless.*

Monday morning, he thumped Wayne in the top bunk bed. 'D'you fancy wagging it today? We could go to the beach, the waves are mint.'

Wayne didn't answer.

'I'll lend you my magnifying glass if you do.' Zac knew Wayne was dying to have a go with it.

'How long can I have it for?'

'Two weeks.'

'If you make it a month, I'll come.' Wayne watched all the nature programmes on telly. He'd like to be an explorer. If he had the magnifying glass, it would be like being one. 'You have to give me the glass before we go to the beach.' He'd been caught out by Zac's promises before.

Zac pulled it out from under his bed and gave it to him. They both got dressed. Wayne dressed slowly; he didn't like doing things with Zac – he always got in trouble – but it'd be worth it for a month's exploring.

It was a wild, windy, blustery day. The tide was in, the sea blasting over the wall.

'Come on, let's run up to the wall and run back when the waves come,' yelled Zac.

'I don't want to get wet, I hate getting wet.'

'Wayne, come on!'

Zac ran forward and back again, laughing as white waves crashed over the wall, soaking the promenade. He was bigger than Wayne and pulled him along. 'Come on, there's no point coming here if you don't come near the wall, don't be a yella belly.'

He yanked Wayne forward as a big wave towered towards them, riding high over the wall. He held on tight to Wayne's jacket.

'Stop it, stop it, I'm soaked. Y'know I can't swim,' screamed Wayne.

The wave loomed above. Zac gave Wayne a big shove forward and ran back to shelter. The last he saw of Wayne was him stumbling, and the giant wave crashing over, swallowing him in white spray.

Wayne breathed in mouthfuls of salty water, the wave knocked him off his feet, lifted him up, smashed him against the wall. His head slapped hard into the cement, his tooth knocked out, lip bleeding, his cheek grazed and bloody. He grabbed hold of a rusty metal bar sticking out from the crumbling wall and held on tight as the waves pummelled him. He cowered, clinging to the rusty rod. Waves crashed, soaking him again and again, pulling him forward and backward like a ragdoll. He'd have been swept away if it hadn't been for the metal bar.

About thirty minutes later, the tide was turning, the waves receding. He lay coughing, unable to get up, soaked through, his teeth chattering. Zac was nowhere. He'd gone.

Very slowly, Wayne shivered his way home. His leg hurt where he'd fallen, his cheek throbbed. When he got in, his lips were blue. He couldn't feel his hands or his feet. He didn't complain or tell on Zac, he knew no one would listen. He hid the magnifying glass in Mr Dobson's old shed. Zac would never think to look in there. Wayne knew he'd try and steal it back.

Zac arrived home an hour later; he'd been on the slot machines. 'Oh shit, you're still alive,' he sniffed. He looked disappointed. Wayne stared at him. Zac slumped on the settee with a bag of crisps to watch TV, and Wayne realised then – Zac was different from other people. He knew if he had died in the sea, Zac would still be on the settee munching his crisps. It wasn't personal – no one mattered. No one. He was like something off the wildlife programmes: unpredictable and very dangerous.

Zac kicked the soldier again. 'Don't be a coward, man. The army hasn't got room for cowards.'

The soldier rolled on the floor. He'd been sick and was clutching his belly. His eye was closing from being knocked against the wall, his ear swelling from where he'd fallen.

'A soldier takes orders, a soldier doesn't question. It is for us to do, not to ask why.' Private Dawson annoyed Zac. He reminded him of Wayne, with his books and his know-it-all attitude. Who the hell did Dawson think he was, asking why? 'If I tell you to shoot, you shoot, whether you think it's right or wrong. If I tell you to jump in a fire – you do it. That's what you're trained to do, you bag of shite.'

Zac stomped down the corridor after teaching that upstart a lesson. He liked the sound of his heavy footsteps echoing in the corridors. He stopped to pull the sleeves of his uniform straight, and to wipe the blood off his shiny boots. He checked the medals pinned on his chest. He polished them every day. He knew he was different from the rest because he was brave; *that's something these cowards can never understand.*

He was a survivor.

tracy's vocation

Nurse Kay told Herbert, 'I don't like people.'

'What? Why are you here? Why are you a nurse if you don't like people? Did I hear right?' Herbert fiddled with his hearing aid.

'You've got egg in your moustache, Herbert.'

'Sorry.' He fumblingly wiped his face, and bits fell onto his tank top. 'Did I hear right, you don't like people?'

'You did.'

'Why?'

'I used to like them. Sometimes it seemed people were nice. Then as I got older, I realised they weren't. Most people are rubbish.'

Herbert nodded. 'You realise a lot as you get older and then you forget. I think maybe I don't like people, but I've forgotten who.'

Nurse Kay sniffed. 'I wish I could forget all the bad buggers I've come across.'

Herbert frowned, unformed faces drifted in his head. Maybe they were the ones he didn't like. Mary had been nice, Mary had been lovely. Herbert's eyes watered. Mary sometimes was here and other times she wasn't. She wasn't like Nurse Kay, with her chewing gum and the mobile phone that she was always looking at. On Fridays, Nurse Kay was happier than usual because she might win the lottery, and 'not have to come to this dump ever again'. Herbert knew it was Friday because they had fish. Herbert hated fish. She'd say, 'Good for your brain cells, Herbert. You might start remembering if you eat your fish.' On Saturdays, she'd be in a worse mood because she hadn't won.

'Why don't you like some people?' Herbert asked.

'What are you talking about, Herbert?' said Nurse Kay over her magazine.

'Didn't you say you used to like people but then they weren't nice, so you didn't?'

'That was yesterday, Herbert. That's a first, you remembering from yesterday, you must've eaten up your fish, after all.'

'Why weren't they nice?'

'Herbert, I'm trying to do my crossword. You're like a dog with a bone. Being let down by people is the story of my life. Take Dave, for example: I thought he was nice, until he ran off with Martha. I thought Gary was lush, and then he turned out to be gay. I thought Brian was lovely until he knocked me about. They're unpredictable, that's the problem with people.'

Herbert rubbed his stubble. Nurse Kay had given him a dreadful shave; definitely no lottery win. 'By people, do you mean males?'

'Oh no, there are some right bitches about – and you can start with my mother.'

'Oh dear.' Herbert couldn't remember Nurse Kay's mother. There was a woman who would sit near the telly, curled into herself like a pink prawn. She either slept all day or was dead, there didn't seem to be much difference. She had the same thick ankles as Nurse Kay; perhaps she was her mother.

Herbert had an accident.

'It's no good saying, "I can't help it," it's me that has to sort you out, you mucky pup.' Nurse Kay had her hands on her hips. She'd shouted at Herbert so everyone knew about the accident.

Herbert's eyes prickled. 'Please let me go home.'

'No, your wife doesn't want you anymore. She says she can't cope.'

Herbert was put into a contraption. It was like a ducking stool hovering over the bath. He sat naked on a sort of toilet seat with his nether regions dangling as Nurse Kay hoisted him up. She plunged him down. Herbert gasped – the water was very cold.

A woman, maybe it was Mary, brought him in a radio. He knew it wasn't Friday because Nurse Kay was extra grumpy. She said words like *shit* and *crap* and *bollocks* – working men's talk.

Herbert fiddled with the radio, but he couldn't fathom out how to work it. A young girl, who looked unhappy and had a red nose, sat next to him. 'Can I talk to you, Herbert? Nurse Kay said you might let me.'

'I expect so,' said Herbert, wondering if it was a test of some sort. They were always doing tests. He didn't think he did very well on them. He rummaged in his pockets for something, but forgot what.

'I'm on work experience.'

'Experience for what work?'

'I'm not sure yet. I think I want to work with animals.'

'I had a dog once, a Labrador, but it died.'

'What did it die of?'

'Old age.' Herbert rubbed his knees, muttering, 'I wish I could die.'

'Don't say that, Herbert. Why are you sad?'

Herbert blinked. 'I can't remember exactly, but I know I am.'

'I'm sad, too. I found out last week my nan's dying. Daft, innit? Here's you wanting to be dead, and there's my nan dying and not wanting to die.'

'What's she dying of?' He couldn't remember who Nan was, but didn't want to seem rude. Herbert thought manners were important for everyone.

'Dunno, exactly. Something to do with her chest.'

The young girl who wanted to work with animals sniffed a lot; she used her sleeve as a hankie. Herbert offered his, but she said, 'No thanks.' She picked her nails for a while and looked at the clock often.

Herbert fiddled with his radio buttons.

'What music do you like?' she asked.

Herbert couldn't remember so pretended not to hear the girl.

'My nan, who I think might be your age, likes big band music. She says she used to go to the dancehalls every Saturday. She tried to show me how to do it, but I've two left feet.'

'Yes, I remember the dancehalls.' It was there and then gone.

The girl shifted in her chair. 'I could bring you in some CDs, if you like. We're sorting through her stuff at the moment. Having a clear out.'

The sniffy, red-nosed girl brought in some CDs the next day. Herbert didn't know what a CD was. The girl said, 'Here, I'll show you, you can play them in your radio.' She pressed the button and *Blue Moon* floated in the air.

Herbert raised his finger and tapped lightly on his chair. 'Ah yes.' He hummed in time with the music.

The girl nudged him and smiled. She wore a metal brace across her teeth. 'See? You do remember.'

He closed his eyes, trying to hang on to the gliding shadows dancing across the parquet floors; the smell of Mary, the touch of her soft skin, her warm hands, her sparkling eyes.

He glanced at the young girl with metal teeth. He wondered where he knew her from. With a lurch of his heart, he hoped she wasn't a grandchild he'd forgotten about.

Nurse Kay stood by the door. 'Go on, Ginger Rogers – show her how it's done. Your Mary says you were proper nifty on your feet when you were younger. You've got trophies and stuff.' Nurse Kay bent over to put nail varnish on a ladder in her tights.

Herbert wondered where these trophies were.

The girl with the metal brace said, 'Go on, Herbert, shall we? I'm gonna die of boredom if I don't do something, I've got to spend two weeks here.'

The music bounced round Herbert's head, little keys unlocked dusty chambers that hadn't danced for years. He shuffled forward from his seat. There was plenty of room in the lounge; the chairs were always pushed up against the wall. His knees creaked as he wobbled and unsteadily stood, but his feet moved with a will of their own, without him having to think. Herbert tapped lightly along a musical tightrope between then and now. He lifted his arms to her. The red-nosed girl awkwardly put her hands on his shoulders as he held her waist. She put one foot on top of the other and almost tripped. She slapped her hand over her mouth giggling. 'Sorry, Herbert, I told you I've two left feet.'

He held her waist gently again, and she put her hand back on his shoulder. He could smell her hair. He led her: 'One, two, three. One, two, three.' Underwater memories floated. 'I'm so glad you've come back.'

She laughed. 'I'm not Mary.' She looked down at their feet, watching her steps, following his lead.

'You must've forgotten. That's always happening to me, too,' he smiled, and for the first time in a long time, it was a big smile. 'Don't you remember how we could dance all night? One, two, three, four. Remember me in my dinner jacket and you in your velvet gown at the Mayfair? We were the business. Don't you remember, Mary?' He mumbled close to her, 'I love you.'

She giggled. 'I'm Tracy.'

'Of course you are.' He gently but firmly led her. 'That's it: round, two, three, four.'

They did three dances in all before Herbert needed a rest. Tracy flopped in the chair next to him, a pinch of colour in her pale cheeks. 'That was ace, Herbert. Can we do it again tomorrow?'

'It would be my pleasure.'

Tracy and Herbert had a little dance every afternoon. Tracy stopped looking at the clock, and Herbert stopped rummaging in his pockets. Tracy popped a CD in the player called *Big Band Music*. 'This is Nan's favourite.'

As they gently whirled across the floor, Tracy asked Herbert with a slight lisp, 'Tell me about the olden days, Herbert, about going to dances and stuff. It'll give me something to talk to Nan about without the cancer being there. When she was young, I know she was happiest dancing.'

As they waltzed and did the cha-cha-cha, Herbert told her about dancehalls, about the girls getting ready and painting lines up their bare legs so they looked like stockings, and about the men putting a cow lick in their hair with a bit of butter. 'All week we waited and worked for Saturday night.'

Tracy told Herbert the next day, 'Nan says you're spot on with what you told me about the dancehalls, Herbert. It's brightened her up talking about it. She sends you her best wishes, by the way.'

'Please return mine.' Herbert once worked with a lady called Jan. The girl had a blocked nose and Herbert thought perhaps that's why she said *Nan* instead of Jan.

On Friday, Tracy helped Nurse Kay to dish out the rubberised squares of fish, swimming in salty milk. 'Ugh, this stinks,' she said, leaning away.

'Here, you can take Ginger Rogers his fish. He looks at me as if I've whacked him with a wet haddock every Friday.'

'You know, Herbert has a fantastic memory, he remembers loads about the olden days,' Tracy said. 'And he remembers all the old dance moves and where to put his feet. He knows all the words to the songs and the tunes. He sings them while we're dancing. He's amazing.'

'Don't be daft, he's away with the fairies. He can't remember his arse from his elbow.'

Tracy raised her chin and took Herbert's plate over to him. She thought Nurse Kay was too stupid to understand about old people. Tracy had decided she wanted to be a nurse instead of working with animals. She'd be good at it, not like Nurse Kay.

'I'm sorry, Herbert, it's fish because it's Friday, but if you eat it quick we can have extra long dancing. I showed Nan the steps you've taught me last night and she thinks you're dead clever.' Tracy bent towards him and dropped her voice. 'I don't think you should be in here, Herbert, you're too good for it. You can talk about history and you can dance like on *Strictly Come Dancing*, and I think you're too much of a gentleman to kick up a fuss, but I don't think you should be here.' Her face flushed indignantly. 'I told my Nan that.'

Herbert nodded. 'Perhaps so.' He'd found that was a good answer to questions or sentences that were perplexing.

She smiled. 'How old are you, Herbert?'

He couldn't remember exactly so guessed. 'I'm one hundred and forty-two.'

Tracy frowned. 'Crikey, I didn't know humans lived that long.'

waiting

Bearded Fran sat astride her stool, peeling waxy potatoes. Her reedy arms swung from her squat body. She looked across the sky, watching a red evening roll in. She was waiting for her cowboy to ride across the horizon. He'd love her fuzzy smallness, and he'd stroke her hairy back. She'd be ten feet tall.

'Day dreaming again, eh, Fran?' said Ringo, passing her caravan.

She grinned. 'One day it'll come true.'

He laughed. 'And I'll win the lottery.'

Fran didn't care for money. It wouldn't make her taller, or less hairy. She dreamt of love, absolute head-over-heels love. She knew it'd happen one day. Gypsy Rosa had seen it in her tea leaves.

She saw him coming out of the big top and her heart galloped, she couldn't take her eyes off him. She wondered what was wrong with him. Everyone that worked at the circus had something wrong with them. She scrutinised his walk – no limp or strange gait. His brown, weathered face had no lumps or bumps; he looked healthy even. He wore an open-neck, checked shirt and denim trousers. His eyes were very blue.

He passed her caravan and nodded. 'Morning.'

She grinned and giggled, giddy with anticipation.

Over lunch, Ringo told the rest of the circus troupe, 'He said he was a mature student finishing off his studies and had a bit of spare time on his hands. He said he wanted to do something practical and short term, to give his brain a rest.'

'Another bleedin' dreamer, then,' said Tania, one of the acrobats.

Ringo sniffed. 'Well, he's not our concern. He doesn't have much to offer, and we're not short of staff at the minute.'

Fran bit her lip. It only took one accident and they would be short-staffed.

The next day, Joe got stomach ache so bad he had to go to hospital.

'Terrible state he's in, they've put one of those drips in him because he can't keep anything down,' said Ringo.

'I reckon it was the cockles he had at Morecambe,' said Myra.

Fran listened and smiled. 'There'll be work for someone, then.'

'Aye, I'll give that bloke a ring.'

She nodded. Joe needed to lose a few pounds.

The man jumped out of the van the next day and waved the driver off. He had high cheekbones and strong features. Fran liked that. She watched him from a distance. Maybe he was one of those getting away from the rat race. The circus had had them before, the ones who couldn't face another day. They usually shacked up in a caravan and tagged on for a week or two, mucking the cages out. Then they got sick of greasy food and went back to where they came from. Some of the drifters were grieving – they'd lost children to drugs, or were recently divorced. They didn't realise grief travels with you. They never lasted long. The worst were the rich, indulged students who'd 'dropped out'. Those long-limbed, healthy, smooth-skinned creatures that moaned, 'I don't feel I belong anywhere.'

'Feckless,' Fran muttered. She wouldn't give that sort the time of day. She spat, 'Not anymore.' They never took any notice of her; she was invisible to them. She wasn't anything special, not like the acrobats or the lion tamer or the clowns. She was just the deformed bearded lady, who also happened to be a dwarf.

She could see the new man was different. Perhaps he'd had a

breakdown, but there were none of the lingering wounds. No nervous tic, no hand wringing, no looking down at his shoes. He walked purposefully, a man who knew what he was doing.

'He's going to paint the wagons and all the woodwork in the big top. Proper handyman, he is,' said Myra the snake charmer, with a greedy glint in her eyes.

He liked Fran's coffee. She gave him a mug at breakfast, one at twelve and one at four. He was quiet; she liked the quiet sort. He nodded, putting his empty coffee mug down, and his blue eyes shone. 'Thanks.'

Myra and Fran sat in the launderette watching the glittery acrobats' frocks go round and round. Myra looked at Fran. 'You're smitten, aren't you?' she teased.

Fran felt her blood surge, she pushed her pinched, small face up close to Myra. 'Mind your own business, Myra, I'm warning you.' Fran had never been in love before, she sat back trembling. This was it, her cowboy in the sunset she'd been waiting for.

Myra looked at her nails. 'He'll be off, Fran. Drifters, they're no good. He'll break your heart, I can tell. He's not interested in a relationship. I think he might be gay.'

Fran turned on her. 'Did he refuse your offer of a few acrobatic flips, eh?'

'Ooohh, who's got it bad?' Myra sniffed.

Fran thought he might be a priest who'd lost his vocation. He had a soulful thoughtful look about him. *Wistful, that's what he is*, she smiled to herself. Sometimes, when Fran handed his coffee over, their hands touched round the mug. She wouldn't wash her hand all day, to keep a bit of him on her.

She knew he wrote every night in his caravan, she'd spied on him tip-tapping on his computer. She imagined poetry and songs. Perhaps he'd sing to her one day.

She made him fairy cakes to go with his coffee, and offered to do his washing for him.

'It's alright, Fran, thanks; I can manage. But we can chat a while, if you like. Tell me about yourself.'

Fran had stayed awake at night trying to prepare her answer to this. If they were going to get married, they needed to know about each other. She thought she might say, 'I was abducted at birth from a wealthy family.' Or maybe something more dramatic: 'I have gypsy blood in me, from a clan with magical gifts.' And she'd stare mistily across the horizon.

But when he asked, she wanted to tell the truth, because that's how they'd be, honest and truthful with one another throughout their lives. 'I've always lived in a circus,' she told him. 'My mother was a bearded dwarf and my dad was one of the acrobats. I wasn't close to either of them. They made me feel as if I was a burden, just another mouth to feed. They both died in a circus fire five years ago. It was a relief, to be honest.'

'Fran, I'm sorry,' he said.

She knew he meant it.

'Did you go to school?' he asked.

'No, no need for that in a circus, and we move around. It's not nice to always be the new one, especially if you're a bit different.'

'So did you get any education?'

'I've learnt everything there is to know about life from working at the circus. I know there are good folk and there are bad. I'm better here than out there. You could say I've a degree in human nature.'

He smiled. 'I'm sure you have. What about friends, did you have anyone to play with?'

'Sometimes seasonal workers would bring their kids and I'd play with them, but they never stayed long. I always had the animals to play with. Nelly is the same age as me. She thinks she's my twin sister by the way she trumpets every time she sees me.'

He smiled again. 'You're very sweet-natured, Fran.'

She put her head to one side. 'Can I show you something?'

'Okay.'

She led him to a small tent next to the big top. In it were mirrors, lots of fairground mirrors. Different distorted images stared back: fat and thin, little and large.

'Stand here,' she said. She stood in front of a mirror next to his. In his reflection, he was squashed small and fat, his face was a troll's grimace. In her mirror, she was elongated, her short limbs were lengthened and stretched. Her round, pug-like face seemed sculptured, her dumpy figure shapely and slim. She pirouetted slowly in the mirror, watching her elegant reflection. 'Now tell me, do you feel any different even though you look different?' she asked him.

'No.'

'Well, neither do I. Look at me in the mirror. I'm the same inside as other women, I have the same desires.' She tried to lock his blue eyes with hers but he looked away mumbling, 'I'm sure you do, Fran.'

She liked the way he whistled quietly as he painted. He was neat and tidy, always cleaned up after himself and put the brushes away. Too soon, he finished the paintwork and Joe came back. Joe was pale, but willing and able. There was no extra work for the man.

'Sorry, mate, I'll have to let you go,' said Ringo.

'No problem, it's been good, thanks.'

'Would you paint my caravan before you go?' Fran asked coyly. 'I can pay you.' She'd emptied out her life savings and counted it all the night before.

He shrugged. 'A couple more days won't make much difference. We can have our last little chat, eh?'

She wanted him to see how tidy and neat her caravan was. He'd realise then what a good wife she'd make. He could move into her caravan and work at the circus. Ringo liked keeping it in the family; that's what he'd be once they married. If he didn't want to roam round the country with the circus, she'd even live in one place with him. A cottage would be nice, somewhere remote. They'd live off the land. At night he'd read to her, their life would be pure and simple. She knew it was what he was looking for.

She baked shortbread.

'Yummm, I love shortbread,' he said, taking another piece with his coffee.

'Me too,' she smiled. 'Isn't it funny how much we've got in common?'

'What do you mean, Fran?'

'Well, we both like shortbread, and we like each other's company, and we like the simple life. All we need is the here and now and each...'

She didn't finish her sentence. He was looking at her, eyebrow raised as if at that moment something had clicked.

Yes, that's right, we are deeply in love. She smiled. *What a sweetheart, it's only just dawned on him.*

'I'd better be off, Fran.' He put his cup down quickly. He didn't look at her as he left.

She sat down and wrote a list of who she'd invite to the wedding. She'd invite the whole circus troupe, even Myra. The trapeze twins could be her bridesmaids. Then she wrote a list of wedding presents. She fell asleep mulling over what she should wear for her honeymoon.

The next morning, it was a bright, blue day. He knocked on her door. 'I was wondering if you fancied a little walk, Fran?'

'Why yes, I'd love one.' She grabbed her cardigan and stepped out of the caravan. He held her hand coming down the steps. They headed down towards the river. Fran felt dizzy. *He's realised he can't fight it. He's going to propose by the river, surrounded by wild flowers and birds singing and the rush of bubbling water.*

He didn't say anything while they were walking. Fran understood: *he's trying to get the words right in his head.* They stepped into a bluebell-carpeted wood. It was shaded and cool.

He cleared his throat. 'I want to thank you very much for everything, Fran. You've made me feel welcome.'

'My pleasure,' she nodded demurely.

'I'm leaving tomorrow. I need to get my thesis handed in.'

Her heart raced. 'Tomorrow?' She stopped in her tracks. *I'll have to break it to him gently that I need at least a week to pack up.* She coughed, trying to give herself time to get her thoughts in order, and asked, 'What's a thesis?'

'A thesis is an academic book. Mine is about travellers. I've been observing and writing up how they live all round the country.' He looked at her. 'Your circus was the last part of the project. I've tried to integrate with each group, living in their community for a short time. I've got all the information I need now, and I'll go back home and write it up. My wife's probably forgotten what I look like.' He laughed gently.

'Your wife?'

'Yes, I have a wife.' He turned to her. 'Fran, our little chats have been particularly helpful – thank you.'

He has a wife. 'Why?' She stamped the ground.

'What do you mean?'

'Why have you tricked us?'

'It's much better if subjects don't know they're being observed. I don't think any harm's been done.'

Fran clenched her fists. 'How we live is no one's business but ours.'

'It's interesting historically and as a social commentary.'

She thought of all the things she'd told him. Hands on hips, she stepped toward him. 'I don't want you to write about me. It's bad enough that people gawp at me day in day out, without them gawping into my life in a book.' She stomped her little, fat legs. 'Never! You are not allowed. You pretended to love me and all the time it was trickery to get your story.'

'Fran,' he said gently, 'I never once exploited you or gave you reason to believe I loved you.'

Fran's eyes narrowed and she jabbed a shaking finger at him. 'You're wicked. You'll get your come-uppance. I'll make sure you do, you'll be sorry, and…' Red-faced, unable to contain her fury, she threw her head back and howled.

He stepped away. 'I'm sorry that's the way you feel, Fran. I'm sorry I'm leaving on a sour note. No one will know it's you, you won't be named and…'

She spat in his face.

He wiped his eye. 'I better go.'

Myra knocked on Fran's caravan that evening after the show. 'We're all having a few drinks at my place. D'you want to come over?'

'No thanks, Myra.'

Myra shrugged. 'Please yourself.'

It was a beautiful summer evening, still and calm. The circus had great takings all week because of the glorious weather. Fran sat on her stool. The laughter from Myra's caravan drifted on a warm breeze. She stared across the orange and red horizon, the same colours the sky had been the night her parents died. She sniffed the whispering summer air. Her skin prickled with gooseflesh, remembering it all.

Later, she watched giggling silhouettes stagger away from Myra's. They fumbled into their caravans to sleep heavily.

They were roughly woken by the crack and cackle of flames in the early hours of the morning. The befuddled circus troupe lurched from their bunks and ran for their lives.

At the inquest it was stated the man had rigged up some dodgy electrical wiring so he could use his computer in the caravan. It was an accident waiting to happen. The circus was exonerated from any blame.

The next site was on soft, green pastures on the outskirts of the town. Fran carried her wash-bag between the caravans. She looked across the horizon and knew one day her cowboy would come riding home. She smiled to herself. 'And when he does, I'll be ten feet tall.'

the leopard

George opened the front door, and closed it quietly behind him. Carol was cleaning as usual. She stopped polishing. 'What did the doctor say?'

'Just a touch of blood pressure, I told you it was nothing.'

'What's he going to do for it?'

'I'll get it checked again in three months.'

'Is blood pressure why you're not sleeping? You did tell him about not sleeping?'

'It's the hot weather, Carol, don't fuss.' George pinched the bridge of his nose. Christ, why couldn't he block it out anymore? For years it had lurked in the recesses of his mind and he'd been able to shove it back into the shadows. Now it was screaming and yelling, ricocheting round his head. 'I'm going for a walk.' He felt a prickle behind his eyes and hurried out before she could argue.

He put his head down and walked fast up the road, trying to leave himself behind. A lorry hurtled by, brushing him in a cold shiver. It tempted him. Sometimes recently he wanted to die, to throw himself in front of a lorry and be done with it all.

He ploughed on despite the heat. It was a hot, humid day. Nowadays everything taunted him with memories from that afternoon all those years ago.

It had been hot and sticky the summer of the *happening*, dank days and sultry nights. Kids his age flaunted themselves in the streets wearing next to nothing. He'd gone for a walk and watched her saunter towards him, teetering on platform shoes that made her legs stretch on forever. He'd never seen her around before. She had long, blonde hair and brown eyes. George was a good-looking lad back then, tall and broad with a lop-sided smile that made the girls giggle. Afterwards he lost the smile. His face hardened to be made of stone.

She'd swaggered her hips in a tight miniskirt, her buttery lips chewing gum as if they were melting. She wore a pink halter-neck top and looked at him full on. *Brazen*, his mother would've called her.

'Have you got the time?' she'd asked, and the way she'd said it could've been – *fancy a fuck?*

'All the time in the world,' he'd teased.

She'd looked up to heaven, swivelling on her long, brown legs. 'Ha, ha. I really need to know the time, my watch has stopped. I'm meant to be meeting someone up here.'

He'd waved his wrist in front of her, teasing. 'Catch me if you can.'

I was young, I was just a kid. That's what he said to himself over and over again. For years he tried to calm himself with platitudes; he hadn't known any better because he was young and foolish.

She'd held her hands up in surrender. 'Fair enough, don't worry, sorry I bothered you. I'll find someone else to ask.' She'd flicked her blonde curls and flaunted past him, muttering, 'Tosser.'

It pissed him off. All that full-on flirting, only to be blown away.

She walked back down the hill, her tight arse wiggling. He guessed she wasn't wearing any knickers. Christ, she was begging for it; his cock twitched.

He jogged after her. 'It's seven fifteen.'

She glanced at him without smiling – 'thanks' – and carried on walking.

He felt a rush of adrenaline and grabbed her arm. 'Don't tell me you only wanted to know the time.'

She flushed angrily. 'Yeah, I only wanted to know the time, now excuse me.' She tried to peel his hand off her arm but he held on tighter, digging fingers into her warm, soft flesh.

'Come on, you can spare a bit of time to spend with me.' George pushed up close. He could smell her perfume.

'Get off me.' She tried to wriggle away, but he held on tighter. She screamed and kicked him with her platform shoe. It stung like hell and made his blood boil. He shoved his hand over her mouth and dragged her into the overgrown bushes. Ham-fisted, face-fucking, he had her; in the fucking ditch, bitch. He rammed his message hard, till she knew and wouldn't forget, on her knees. He was seriously pissed off with prick teasers like her.

He left her there, maybe alive or dead, he didn't care. He went home and took the stairs two at a time straight up for a shower. He was annoyed he'd got dirty from the muck. He threw the clothes away and scrubbed hard, but was never clean again. His mum shouted up, 'Your tea's ready.'

He went downstairs, smiled, and sat at the table to begin his new pretend life.

He tried to convince himself over the years that he was a decent human being. That it had been a moment's madness he had to learn to live with. He survived day to day, hour to hour. With time, it became a bad dream instead of a waking nightmare. Now, after all those years, it was catching up with him. Simple things like fixing the kitchen drawer last week could trigger a panic attack. He'd slipped with his Stanley knife and a thin smile on his hand grinned back in blood, so red like her slash of crimson lipstick. After all those years, it was as if he was staring into her face again.

Mr Dunne was walking his dog across the park. 'Enjoying retirement, George?' he shouted.

'It's taking some time getting used to, but early days yet.' He didn't stop, he wanted to walk and walk and never stop. He headed for Winters Hill. He wanted space and solitude. He often went there nowadays, to tempt fate. He could trip and fall head first onto the rocks – it would be an accident. He knew Carol would get over it. She had lots of friends and they'd rally round her. She'd got used to him hardly ever being there. She was involved in the church, flower arranging and cleaning pews. George had tried religion, but couldn't raise his eyes to the crucifix – or any god. He knew he was damned.

Work had saved him. He worked twenty-four-seven and only reluctantly took holidays when urged to. Even then, he arranged a busy programme of activities for the whole break. He'd fought the redundancy tooth and nail, but lost.

He pushed on up the hill. The summer air was heavy with scent, flowers wilted in the heat. A trickle of sweat ran between his shoulder blades. He would change his shirt when he got back, probably change all his clothes. He'd got fastidious after it happened, he couldn't bear to smell or be dirty. He'd scrub and scrub himself raw, trying to wash himself away.

George kicked a stone. His head throbbed. He glanced up from the ground and saw an office girl. She was sitting on a bench at a viewpoint on the hill, drinking a Coke and eating her sandwich. She looked up at him and his heart stopped: blonde hair; brown eyes; long, lovely legs. He stared back to thirty years ago.

She raised an eyebrow. 'What?' She had the same *come on* look.

'You look...' he stuttered. 'You look just like someone...' He coughed. '...someone I once knew.'

She shrugged, and took a bite of her sandwich. He watched her pink lips. He stared until she raised an eyebrow again, 'You're making me feel uncomfortable.'

'Your mother, how is your mother?'

'Do I know you?' she asked sharply.

'No, no, you're the spitting image of someone I once knew. Do you look like your mother?' He hadn't realised he'd stepped towards her. He was bearing down on her, his voice raised a notch. Maybe this was his chance, maybe he could redeem himself and say sorry.

He'd give her money, lots of money. He'd try to get her to forgive him and then he could forgive himself.

He didn't mean to frighten the girl, but he was standing so close, his eyes so wide, sort of excited. A flick of spittle flew as he was talking, talking too fast.

She didn't like him and there were no other people around. She grabbed her bag and started running down the hill – the pathetic, penguin-flapping run that women in heels do. She left her magazine. He picked it up and jogged after her. 'Wait, wait, I don't mean you any harm.'

As she ran, she looked back; her face full of fear, her legs and arms moving as if made of rubber. He caught up with her and grabbed her arm, the same soft, warm flesh. If he could just reason with her, if she'd listen, she could save him.

She opened her mouth wide and screamed. She reached out and clawed his face, kicking him hard. His shin seared pain. He panicked, shaking her. 'Stop it! I don't mean to harm you. I just want to talk...'

She screamed louder, windmill arms and legs hitting out, nails clawing, teeth biting, falling fists. He pressed his hand against her mouth to calm her, to make her listen.

She wouldn't listen. He pressed harder and harder, dragging her down into the dark, deep ditch.

After, in her silence, he could hear earthworms burrowing. Her eyes were open, so he closed them.

wiggy

I get the bus to school and so does my thick brother. We disown each other once we step out of the house; I go upstairs on the bus, he goes down – we keep it that way. Sharon gets on at Blackpool Tower. My dad says she's a bad influence, but she's a good laugh, and I don't get much of that at home. Mum tried to split us up at the beginning of term by asking the teachers to separate us, but we drifted back together on the wrong side of bad. No one seemed to notice. We sit at the back of class being bored. If you're at the very back of class, the teachers lay off. They only consider bothering about you if you're second row from the back. The back is damnation to NVQs, almost special needs. Their eyes glaze over, they can't be arsed.

I have to change my shoes on the bus upstairs. I've bought some four-inch platforms out of my own money. Mum refused to buy them but I don't care if they wreck my back – I look a babe. The first day I wore them, Mr Mason yelled, 'Do not wear them to school again.' So I have the pleasure of my platforms for the bus journey, but then have to do a flamingo impression, jiggling on one leg while I change into plimsolls at the school gate. I keep them in my bag because the poxy prefects get their kicks dobbing me in.

'Double history and double maths,' I moan to Sharon as we walk up to class. 'I think I'm losing the will to live.'

Sharon grabs my arm. 'Oh my God, look at Maureen! Oh God, it is Maureen, isn't it?'

Maureen's a mouse girl who sits in the corner. You'd never notice her if wasn't for the fact that Sharon treats her like a dog she can kick every time she sees her. Let's just say she has *issues* with her.

'Oh my God. I mean, oh my God.' Sharon squeezes my arm tighter. 'Look, she's got a wig on.'

It's a terrible wig, a stiff helmet bob, like a Lego man.

'Why?' I say quietly. 'Why the hell would she wear a wig?' I try to remember what Mouse looked like before the wig. It's a pale, hazy image; maybe her hair is slightly ginger. Sharon giggles hysterically; I can see other girls giggling, too. Mouse scuttles by, her head down.

Sharon's electric, the wig has plugged her in. She lights up in history and even grins through double maths. She keeps nudging me with doodles of Mouse, and flicks little balls of paper across the room to hit her so she'll turn round and we can have a good gawp at the helmet. When Mouse puts her head down to write you can see where the wig ends and real hair tufts stick out. Sharon snorts and pretends it's a sneeze. She gets me going and we nearly pop trying to keep all the giggles gagged. When the bell for goes for lunch, Sharon jumps up. 'Oh, I've got to see this close up.'

Maureen's already beetled out of class, and nowhere to be seen.

She's back in class in the afternoon. Sharon's eyes widen like she's hunting an endangered species. After last lesson when the bell goes, Mouse scrapes up her bag and is gone – vamoose. We hurtle down to the cloakroom but she's nowhere. We run to the bus stop to try and catch up with her, shoving and pushing as usual. Sharon's wicked with the lower school; they're terrified of us. We sit up on top of the double decker bus mouthing off. I'm trying to sneakily change into my platforms, ferreting round in my gym bag, when

Sharon screeches, 'There, there. Look, she's there.' She stands up on the seat and pulls the window open. Sharon doesn't care who sees her knickers. 'Hey, Wiggy. Wiggy!' she yells.

Mouse doesn't look up. She keeps her head down and for a fleeting second I feel sorry for her, Sharon's such a cow. She flops back down howling with laughter and I throw my head back and cackle too. Sharon gets off three stops before me, so I've time to calm down. I teeter down the bus holding onto bars of the seats. One of the old bags at the back glares at me and says, 'No excuse for that kind of behaviour.'

I know Sharon would've stared her out or given her some lip, but I'm not so brave and look away. I take the platform shoes off at the lamppost on our corner because Mum would start on me if she knew I wore them to school. Sometimes, just the thought of seeing Mum and Dad irritates me, and if my stupid brother is more moronic than usual, I might run away with Sharon, like she's always saying we should.

Mum's in the kitchen being busy doing not very much. 'Did you have a nice day, dear?' she asks while dialling someone up on the phone.

'Yeah, there was an axe-wielding madman who ripped through half my class, which helped pass the time of day.'

No answer. I knew she wasn't listening. Basically, they all suck.

The next day, Maureen's off sick. No one knows why, and no one would care if it hadn't been for the wig. Then I get the shock of my life in double English when Mrs Soames says, 'Now, Louise, I'd like to discuss your essay…'

I think, *Oh no, this is going to be a detention*, but she says 'It's a wonderful piece of descriptive work.' I'm mortified as she says, 'I'd like to share it with the class.' And she reads it out. Sharon's sulky, she hates it if I do well, it's like I'm being disloyal to her. Mrs Soames raves on and on about my essay. I could die of embarrassment but in my heart I'm chuffed to bits.

When I get in, I'm buzzing to tell them about the essay but Mum has her friend Carol round and they're going to the cinema. I wait for Dad to get in from work, he doesn't get back until late. I can tell he's dead tired but can't wait to tell him. He has his tea on a tray and is watching TV when I bring him my essay. 'She read it out to the whole class. I'll read it to you.'

I start reading. 'Very good,' he says randomly, but doesn't stop watching the TV, or lifting the fork to his mouth. When I stop reading halfway through the essay, he just sits staring and doesn't seem to notice I've stopped. I look at him wondering when it is that adults transform from normal functional beings to miserable gits, and women with sheep brains and woolly hair. He's not been listening, he can't be bothered. My eyes prickle. It must mean nothing to him; I mean nothing. I slam my book shut and run upstairs. I leave the curtains open and watch the sky change colours. I can't wait to grow up and get away from this shithole.

The next day, I wake full of fury. Stuff him, I hate them all. I slam the front door so hard the pane of glass nearly drops out. I meet Sharon at the school gates. She's having a smoke and drags on her ciggy as if it's an inhaler. Her eyes are burning; she's on a mission. 'Let's get Wiggy today.'

'What d'you mean?'

She grinds her fag out. 'Let's get the wig off and see what's underneath.'

'Leave her be, Shaz.' I try coaxing her, but Sharon has that glint in her eye. It's all to do with Maureen's auntie Belinda, who according to Steph Wilson, ran off with Sharon's dad. It's nothing to do with Maureen, but for months Sharon's been taking it out on her; she's legged her up in the dinner queue, knocked into her in the corridor and slags her off any chance she gets. I don't want to look under Maureen's wig, there might be something gross underneath, a disgusting rash or minging disease, and Maureen's never done me any harm.

But Sharon's high as a kite and won't listen. She links my arm and drags me along. 'C'mon, let's go and find Wiggy.'

We hunt for her down the corridors, in the classrooms, up to the IT block, round the cloakrooms and eventually find her cowering in the toilets. I liked the screeching round corners, and running about like loonies looking for her, but once I see her shivering in a corner of the stinky loo, her vinyl-looking wig slightly skew-whiff, I feel cold and wish we hadn't found her.

Sharon swaggers up to her. Maureen's white with fear, I can see her shaking. I look at Sharon and my belly tightens. I don't want to be here. I pull Sharon's arm. 'C'mon, Shaz, leave her. She's not worth the bother.'

She turns to me, her mouth all twisted. 'What's your problem? Scared?'

I feel sick and say, 'I think someone might come and you've scared her enough.'

Sharon ignores me and steps towards her. Maureen crouches down.

'I just want a little peek under that wig.'

I pull her sleeve. 'C'mon, Shaz.'

She turns, glaring. 'Why don't you fuck off?' She pushes me back and leaps forward, pouncing on Maureen. She shoves her knee into her chest, pinning her down, grabbing for the wig. She scratches Maureen's face, who's twisting and turning wildly trying to hold onto the wig, her face red, her mouth open wide, her eyes rolling marbles. I freeze. I'm turned to stone watching Maureen's head banging against the wall. Sharon's laughing, the wig shifting back and forward as if her head's been ripped off. Maureen screams and screams then Sharon suddenly falls back with the helmet clutched in her hands. Maureen throws her arms up trying to cover her head up, howling so loudly it cracks my frozen glass. I break free and run. I run with my hands over my ears to stop Maureen's screaming. I run so I can't see Sharon waving her wig and kicking her. I run so no one can see me crying.

I go and sit in the library. Maureen's terrified face swims before me again and again. When the bell goes, I go straight to class and sit near the front, feeling lonely. I wait for Maureen to come in, but she doesn't. I ignore Sharon.

At home-time, she's waiting for me with a couple of her sidekicks. She sneers, 'You're a fucking coward.'

Her cling-ons snigger.

'So you're suddenly Wiggy's best mate?' Sharon taps her foot.

I spit back, 'What's your problem, Sharon? It's not Maureen's fault your dad left.'

Sharon lunges at me. It's a feathers flying, snatching, kicking, biting, hair-pulling, bitchy fight. I run home and never want to see that cow again.

The next day, I get the bus early and don't wear my platforms. I want a don't-notice-me day, which is tough titty because first thing I'm called to Mr Mason's office. He looks grim. 'I've called you in today to discuss some serious allegations of bullying…'

Dad takes me to hospital to see Maureen. She took an overdose after Sharon had done with her. We walk down the sweaty green hospital corridors; my shoes sound very loud. She's in ITU, unconscious. The unit is bright and glaring. Maureen's surrounded by machines, they bubble and gurgle; a windmill of nurses whirl round, clicking, ticking, pricking. Maureen's skin is greyish white and I wonder whether she has any blood left inside. She has wires tangling inside and out of her, and a plastic tube in her mouth. Her wig is on the locker beside her bed; it looks like a dead animal. Maureen's head is virtually bald. I can see the tiny blue veins on her skull. I swallow down the lump in my throat, my eyes are blurry.

After a while, Dad says, 'Why on earth did you get mixed up in this?'

My mouth is dry. I can't talk in case I start blubbing.

He says, 'Maureen's hair fell out because she was bullied at school and she was so scared. The incident yesterday was the final straw.'

A nurse comes in to check on Maureen and stares at me. I hate her; she makes me feel guilty. I hate my dad for the way he looks at me. I hate Sharon for making her do it. I hate everyone at school for the way they looked at me when I left Mr Mason's office. I hate Mum for crying and my dumb brother for smirking. Most of all, more than anyone, I hate myself.

between a rock and a hard place

'So, why?'

'Why what?' said Josie, shifting her rucksack on to her other shoulder.

'Why are you doing the Santiago de Compostela pilgrimage?' asked Mark. 'Everyone does it for a reason.'

Josie had promised herself she wouldn't moan. She was determined to do it without help; she'd be a proper pilgrim. Three weeks – that's all they'd give her off work. Three weeks to get back on track. For once in her life, she'd finish what she set out to do.

'I'm doing it to get my head sorted.'

Mark nodded. 'Ah, a head sorter. I won't ask any more, then.'

Josie smiled at him. 'Thanks. Why are you doing it?'

'I did the walk when I was about the same age as you, twenty years ago now. I lost the love of my life and my dad died unexpectedly. I suddenly wasn't sure what I was living for. I was in a well-paid job, but lived only to get out of my skull on a Friday night. So I gave it all up, came here, thought a bit, and went back and re-trained as a teacher. It's not perfect, but better.'

'So why are you doing it again?'

'It gave me a different perspective on life.' He smiled. 'I think I need a refresher course in how to be human.'

They were interrupted by a middle-aged man bumping Josie's rucksack as he barged past. His wife scurried behind.

'Woah' – Mark reached out to steady Josie – 'someone's in a hurry.'

They watched the bulbous man blunder ahead with no apology.

His wife struggled along, trying to keep up. *Sorry*, she mouthed to Josie.

'What's the rush?' Mark muttered as the couple disappeared round the next corner.

Josie gave an empty laugh. 'He's the sort I want to get my head round. I seem to have become bitter and twisted towards my fellow man.'

'Hmm.' Mark winked. 'Definitely in need of some head sorting. I'll catch you later. I'm having a comfort break here.'

'See you,' she said, waving.

Josie walked. The weather was perfect, warm with a light breeze. She nodded to a couple she'd seen at breakfast and they nodded back; middle-aged and preoccupied. She watched them plodding, heads bowed, heavy-legged. They were carrying sadness. She wondered if they'd lost a child, or if someone in their family was ill. Everyone who did the Santiago de Compostela did it for a reason. There was comfort in that.

Josie tried to see herself through their eyes: a thirty-year-old woman walking alone. If it wasn't their first guess, it'd be their second. Break-up of a relationship was fairly predictable. Maurice had done the *I know we get on so well, but…* as kindly as he could, while stabbing her through the heart. If she thought about it for too long, she couldn't catch her breath. She went through the motions of work and friendships, but her broken heart was bleeding her dry.

It was strange that a priest had suggested the walk. He'd been visiting the gallery where she worked. He'd asked about a Spanish painting displayed. He'd said, 'It reminds me of the scenery along the Santiago de Compostela walk.'

'Where's that?' she'd asked.

'It's in Spain. It's a pilgrimage, but you don't have to be religious to do it. It's more of a spiritual journey' – he'd smiled – 'a renewal of self.'

She liked the way the lines danced round his eyes. Typical of her luck that he was a priest.

That evening she'd googled the walk and booked it. Her friends thought she was crazy. 'Three weeks, Josie? You'll only have two weeks' annual leave left.'

'You're in danger of becoming a nun. I'm worried about you.'

'Don't be.'

Post-Maurice, people irritated her. On the commute home, people pushed and shoved. They scowled. They talked too loud or picked their noses. Couples argued, kids whined. Josie grieved for the happy-go-lucky self she used to be.

The first third of the Santiago de Compostela was a dream. She was immersed in a good world. No TV, no email, no computer, no having to have a conversation. Instead there was space, silence, rolling hills, gentle smiles. The hostels were run by kind people. They served stews and hotpots and casseroles. People chatted in different languages. She'd walk for an hour or two with one group, then another, sometimes with couples, sometimes with loners.

The angry walrus-man and his browbeaten wife seemed to pop up most days, taunting her. As soon as Josie saw them, her eyes narrowed and the hairs on the back of her neck bristled. Josie had seen the woman trying to engage him in conversation, but he ignored her, spending meal times on his laptop. She winced watching him dismiss his wife with a flick of his hand. The woman gave up and stared into space.

The second week was hell. The terrain was bleak and bare. The barren land stretched on and on. The wind blew, the skies were grey. People moaned and groaned. Blisters and food poisoning were common. It rained often. She felt damp and sticky and at night she was cold. The hostels were fewer and further between. The hostel owners were tight-lipped and unfriendly, the beds small and lumpy. The local accents were so guttural they were difficult to understand. The showers were cold, the food inadequate and bland.

'This is the real pilgrimage,' the man fog-horned one morning, masochistically grinning as he marched past Josie, again knocking her shoulder.

Josie talked to few people in the second week. She kept her head down, determined not to grumble. She was permanently tired, hungry and thirsty. She hoped she'd lost some weight.

Towards the third section, she met Mark again.

'The third section is beautiful,' he said. 'It's the best.' He swallowed a hunk of bread and looked around the rolling countryside. 'I like that the pilgrimage reaffirms what really matters in life. First, the basic requirements: food, warmth, shelter; and then somehow while walking, it makes you think of the bigger picture – what matters at a deeper level.'

Josie nodded. She'd learnt on the walk it was often better to say nothing.

'And Josie. Young, beautiful Josie. What about you?'

'My head is getting a bit sorted,' she smiled.

'Ahh.'

'I'm still trying to pick myself up, brush myself down and re-adjust my attitude, but since I've split with my ex, it seems I have a problem' – she shrugged – 'I don't like many people.'

Mark laughed. 'Life – it's not what you see, it's the way you see it.'

'I want to re-discover my sunshine smile. I still wake up frowning, in a bad mood.'

'That's a shame, because you have a lovely smile. It's a mistake to rely on one person for your happiness, it's a big ask.'

'I know,' she sighed. 'Too big.'

Mark nodded to a small café. 'I'm stopping for a bite to eat, care to join me?'

'No thanks, I had lunch half an hour ago.'

'Okay, bye for now.'

She watched him walk off, wishing he was twenty years younger and didn't smell of cheese.

The walk became lushly green and peaceful. Other walkers smiled and she smiled back, they were nearly there. Josie's pace was brisk. She felt a flutter of excitement; she'd done it, and she'd done it alone.

At the next hostel, the bulldog-man was there. He was on his laptop while his wife stared. She seemed to have become completely mute. Josie wondered what thoughts went on behind those vacant eyes. She caught the wife's eye. The woman gave a quick smile and glanced across the table – as if she might get reprimanded.

Josie played with the sugar in her cup before pushing it away and setting off. She walked and walked and tried not to think. She was done with thinking. She breathed deeply. *Enough. It's time to move on.*

Mark caught up with her. 'This section is gorgeous, isn't it?'

'It really is.' They fell in to walking together and came to a stream. The sun danced through the trees. The water was clear and bright. She bent and cupped the cold mountain water in her hands, drank and drank again. She wiped her mouth and was ready to set off when the stone caught her eyes. It shone under the water, bright lights bouncing from it. She bent and lifted it. It was different shades of blue and orange, shot with sparkling silver and green. She turned it over. The more she looked at it, the more colours she saw; a glint of a fish eye, a flash of slippery scales. It seemed alive.

She lifted it in both hands to show Mark. 'Isn't it wonderful?' She looked down at the swirling colours. 'I'd love to keep it, but it should stay here – so all walkers passing through can enjoy its beauty.'

'Josie, keep it,' Mark smiled. 'You don't have to beat yourself up about everything.'

'No, I'll put it back, that's the right thing to do. It might give me luck.'

'If it makes you feel better,' he said, shrugging.

She kissed the stone and whispered, 'To the future,' and dropped it into a cold, deep pool. The ripples moved as if the stone was waving.

That night, she lay awake for a long time. She got up and sat at the window; she felt better and stronger and happily watched clouds skit across the moon.

The next day, she walked with Mark again. He rubbed his feet. 'Nearly there now.'

'Yeah, it's been a long journey.'

He nodded. 'It's not been as easy as the first time, I feel knackered.'

Josie sighed. 'I think that's like love. First time is easy, isn't it? Second time will be harder.'

'Atta girl, but there will be a second time.'

They stopped for a coffee and the browbeaten wife and bulldog-man sat at a table nearby. He clicked his fingers impatiently for her to pass the salt.

'See, that's the trouble,' said Josie. 'Back in the real world there are so many selfish gits like him around. They bring out the worst in me.'

'Ah, give him some slack. He was maybe bullied as a kid, and it's the only way he knows.'

'Maybe, and maybe I'll never be as generous-hearted as you.'

They sipped their coffee, enjoying the sun.

The man's voice boomed across the café: '...and I got this little beauty in one of the creeks.'

Josie's heart missed a beat. She leant forward. 'The stone, he's got the stone,' she hissed.

'Josie, it's a stone,' shrugged Mark. 'Look on the bright side, it's heavy and he has to carry it.'

'But I put it back for everyone to enjoy, not him...'

The wife saw Josie watching and looked down into her lap.

'It was my stone,' Josie fumed.

'Josie, it wasn't anyone's stone.' Mark patted her hand.

'Mark, don't you ever think human nature sucks?'

'All the time,' he smiled.

'Don't you ever feel like hitting out at all the ignorant bastards like him who push themselves forward' – she slapped the table – 'trampling on everyone else?'

'Not anymore.'

At the city of Santiago, a wave of pilgrims hobbled towards St James's cathedral. It was the end of the pilgrimage. Josie wasn't religious but wished she could be more spiritual. She shook her head; no more wishing.

Inside the cathedral, it was opulently ornate, heavy with gold and jewels, polished marble and mosaics. She sat on a cool, wooden bench and tried to pray. *Help me be more tolerant, more accepting, more forgiving. To see people in a better light. To give them the benefit of doubt.*

Josie's prayers were interrupted by the pompous man stomping noisily up to the front. He took photos, rudely blocking the view of people trying to pray at the altar. Josie felt her body stiffen with outrage. A monk approached the man and asked him quietly to stop taking photographs. The man barked and ignored the monk, continuing to snap his camera. Eventually, he sat in the front bench and snorted loudly. A few minutes later his wife crept apologetically up the aisle.

Instead of going in next to her husband, she slipped into the bench behind him. The woman bowed her head low, and then lifted her face to the crucifix. Josie wondered if she was praying for the strength to put up with her husband. The woman stared transfixed at the cross, her lips moving with prayer. After blessing herself, the woman bent to rummage in her bag.

Josie saw the colours dancing. The woman held the stone reverently in both hands, as if it was sacred. Josie watched the woman raise her eyes upward with the stone, high above her head – an offering to the all-forgiving God – before whispering, 'God help me.' After thirty years of marriage, the woman smashed the weight down on her husband's head, cracking his skull wide open.

quality of life

John rubbed his eyes. He'd been on call for forty-eight hours and spent nearly all of it with baby Jones in the Special Care Unit. Roxanne, the young mum, smiled wearily as he left. 'We're going to call him John, after you. Thank you for saving his life.' She hugged him tight.

He hadn't, but was too tired to argue. He looked at Roxanne and Jason holding hands over their son's cot.

'He looks so perfect,' said Jason. He bit his lip and asked again, 'He'll be alright, won't he?'

John pulled up a chair so he wasn't looking down at the young couple; they made him feel old. He tried to explain. 'Sometimes there's an obvious reason why babies don't do well, but sometimes we never find out. I can't say exactly what's wrong with your baby, but it's early days. We'll do the best we can for him.'

'Do you think he'll be okay?' Roxanne begged for the magical *yes.*

'I don't know until we have a proper diagnosis, but he's a little fighter.'

Roxanne's mother Dawn arrived. 'Oh Roxy, congratulations. My first grandson. Why is he here on the Special Care Unit?'

'There's something wrong with him, Mam.'

Dawn peered into his cot. 'What's wrong with him? He looks perfect. Why's he got all those wires?'

'They don't know yet.' Roxanne glanced at John. 'He won't breathe properly.'

Dawn straightened up, facing John squarely. Her eyes narrowed. 'Are you the baby doctor?'

'I'm looking after your grandson, yes.'

'So what's wrong with him?'

'We're doing tests.'

John's bleeper went. 'I'm sorry, I have to go. I'll catch up with you two later.'

After he'd re-sited the intravenous infusion in Nina Wall on Ward 14, he went back to baby John for a final check before going off duty for the weekend.

Sister Sheila said, 'I think the baby is doing a little better than a couple of hours ago.' She smiled at John; she was always optimistic. You couldn't work on the Special Care Unit if you didn't believe in miracles.

John watched the baby kick and wave his arms, swinging balled fists against the life he'd been landed with. John sighed and said, 'He's still going to need ventilating.'

John went off duty, pulling his tie and undoing his top shirt button as he went. He met Marcus in the corridor. 'Hey Marcus, are you on call this weekend?'

'Yeah, unfortunately, I'm getting too old for this lark.'

'There's an interesting case on the Special Care Unit. A normal antenatal history with an uneventful delivery, but almost immediately the baby was in trouble. Some slight webbing of hands and feet but most worrying is the respiratory distress; he's struggling to breathe. There's no recognisable syndrome that I know of. The anaesthetist is there now ventilating him.'

Marcus yawned. 'Great, just what I need. Are the parents aware of all this?'

'I've tried to put them in the picture. They're very young, in shock, I think. I'm not sure they've taken in a word I've said.'

'It's getting better and better.'

'And be careful with the grandmother; she's feisty.'

Marcus grimaced. 'John, why do I get all the luck?'

John patted his shoulder, laughing. 'You must've been wicked in a previous life.' He waved. 'Have a good weekend and don't work too hard.'

Marcus watched John saunter down the corridor whistling quietly. John never seemed to question what they were doing, never got tired of playing God; thumbs up or down to life. Marcus's head pounded, he was hungover again. He stepped heavily, trudging along the corridor. It seemed uphill, his thighs twitched, he was tired and hungry. The line between making a difference to people's lives and simply meddling was blurring. Mother Nature was smarter than medicine. Recently, Marcus wanted to pay more respect to this. He was sick of trying to save hopeless cases, condemning some poor kid to a half brain-dead existence.

He headed for the crazy, mixed-up world of Ward 10. In Bed 4 was a petrified Mrs Dawson on bed-rest. It was her third pregnancy; she'd lost the other two at about five months, this time she was at six and a half months gestation. In Bed 5 was Bev, one of their regulars, in for her fourth termination. The two women chatted about morning sickness.

John drove slowly. He was tired and thinking about baby John. The miracle of life never ceased to amaze: warm, soft skin; a beating heart; a new life. Even an imperfect one was exquisite. The baby had fluttered muddy, watery eyes, unfocused. John had stared, holding a fellow human being swimming upstream while he examined him. He was struggling to survive.

Marcus introduced himself to Jason and Roxanne. An older, blonde woman scowled at him. 'I'm the baby's grandmother. What's all this about something wrong with him?'

'I'm on duty for the weekend and I'll be looking after baby,' Marcus said. 'I'd like to examine him first.'

'Well, I hope we'll have some answers soon, that other doctor didn't tell us anything proper.'

'Mam, don't.' Roxanne looked tearful.

'We've had to give him a bit of extra help with his breathing,' said Marcus.

'Why?' said the grandmother, crossing her arms.

'Because he's not managing on his own.'

'He looks alright to me. If you don't know what's wrong with him, how do we know there's anything wrong with him, eh? I've had five kids and he looks right as rain to me.'

Marcus bit the inside of his mouth. 'Well, he isn't.'

Baby John was wired up and plumbed in. He'd been given muscle relaxants so he couldn't thrash and flail. The parents sat either side of the incubator. 'Will he be alright?'

Marcus focused on the baby. It was easier than looking at their pleading eyes. 'We don't know, sometimes this happens. A child totally flummoxes the textbooks and is an unknown quantity.'

John sighed at the traffic lights. In all honesty, he knew the odds were stacked against baby John, but there were exceptions to every rule. It was the million-to-one shot that made this job worthwhile, the ones that against all odds made it. He thought of the flicker of hope in the baby's smoky eyes, a connection; he looked like a fighter. A car beeped behind, the lights changed; John was exhausted, he needed to concentrate. A weekend away from the hospital would recharge his batteries. He'd switch off, have a nice meal and bottle of wine with Maria. They'd have a lazy lie-in. Maria wanted to shop for a new sofa, he'd see how he felt. He turned into their driveway. He knew he'd ponder over baby John, he hoped for him.

Marcus burped quietly; he had nauseous, post-booze heartburn. He stared at the little body of baby John, his chest going up and down, the map of fine blue veins he could trace under his skin. He felt a hopeless futility creep into his heart. Recently, he felt it often.

Marcus spent a long time with the parents. 'No one can predict how your baby will do.' He talked slower. 'We don't know exactly what's wrong with him, but he doesn't seem able to breathe unaided.'

'The other doctor seemed to think things were a bit better than you're saying,' Roxanne snivelled.

Marcus looked at his shoes. *Bloody sunshine John.*

John un-clicked the door, the smell of home-baked lasagne and the racket of Danny's music throbbed through the house. He could see Maria in the kitchen and heard her talking to Steph. 'You've got to be back by midnight or I'll ground you for a month.'

'I will, Mum, take a chill pill.' Steph flounced past John. 'See you later, Dad.'

He watched her swagger out in a tiny micro skirt. 'Bye, sweetheart,' he muttered to the closing door. In the kitchen he kissed Maria. 'D'you think that skirt's a bit short for her?'

She patted his hand. 'Get over it, Daddy.'

Marcus's bleeper went off all night. He was called out to a difficult twin delivery; one baby lived, the other died. Then he was called out to Mrs Dawson. She was hysterical, she'd started bleeding. The obstetrician had arrived and listened to her belly. He locked eyes with Marcus, giving a small shake of his head.

Marcus blinked and looked at Mrs Dawson. 'I'm sorry.' He turned away.

At 6am, he lay down on the small on-call bed. The room was white and bare, the narrow bed unruffled, he'd been up all night. He was so tired. He took a sip of vodka from his inside pocket and closed his eyes. A minute later his bleeper went off. Blank-eyed and bleary, he looked out the window at the clawing morning sunlight. He realised he didn't look forward to anything in life anymore, except sleep.

The bleep was a call from the Special Care Unit. 'Baby John's parents want to speak to you,' said the nursing sister.

Roxanne and Jason looked exhausted. The randomness of bad luck shot through them. Marcus stood over them, one either side of baby John's cot. He looked at the little frame inside, the creased skin of the child's crumpled face; he was an old man in a baby's body.

'What's going to happen?' asked Jason.

'We'll keep monitoring the situation.' Marcus stifled a yawn.

They had a hollowed, empty look of grief. They were carrying the loss of a perfect newborn baby, and the possible life sentence of caring for a severely handicapped son. They watched their baby, trying to absorb his pain so he wouldn't suffer. Marcus watched them – the adult of the species trying to always protect their young. In nature, it was survival of the fittest.

Jason pulled his tired eyes away from his son. His voice scratched the air. 'We don't want him to suffer.' He put his finger into the incubator and stroked his son's slightly deformed fingers. Jason stared at Marcus. 'I mean, if he needs a ventilator for the rest of his life' – he shrugged – 'that's no life.' He wiped his eyes with a rough brush of his thumb.

Marcus pulled up a chair. 'It's difficult without a diagnosis. We don't know if he'll improve or not, it's not a recognised syndrome.'

'Christ, doc, he can't breathe, that's not compatible with life. What are we trying to do here?' Jason's eyes swam with desperation.

Roxanne whispered, 'We don't want him to suffer anymore.'

Marcus looked at baby John and away quickly. 'We could take him off the ventilator and see how he does?'

Marcus knew they were both young, both stupid, they'd do what he suggested. He was so tired, he could maybe get a couple of hours sleep before handover. They both looked back at the ventilated child and nodded.

Baby John died in his parent's arms peacefully half an hour later. They cradled him together, crooning. All his wires were undone, he was free. They listened to the hush. Roxanne touched his lips with hers, her ear pressed up close to his silence.

John drove in on Monday morning, humming. It had been a good weekend – nothing special, pottered in the garden, had a nice meal and bottle of wine, they'd bought a new sofa, Maria was happy. He parked and whistled his way across the car park. It'd be interesting to see how baby John was doing; he hoped he continued to improve.

He met Marcus on the stairs. 'Hi Marcus, how was your on-call? You look knackered.'

Marcus shrugged. 'Not good.'

'Oh, while I remember' – John clicked his fingers – 'are you and Carole still okay for next Saturday night?'

'Yeah, great.' Marcus glanced at his feet. He'd have to tell John sometime that Carole had left him three weeks ago, but not now, not yet.

'How's baby John? Interesting case, I thought.'

Marcus shook his head. 'I'm afraid he didn't make it. The parents requested he be taken off the ventilator.'

John felt a kick in his belly. 'You took him off? Why the hell? He seemed to be improving.'

'Come on, John, a slight improvement but his prognosis was awful. We might have eked out another week of agony. As it was, he died at rest with his parents. It's what they wanted. For once I felt I did a good thing instead of creating misery.'

John fumed, 'I can't believe you did that. It's too early, even a day or two more…'

Marcus yelled, 'We're not gods, John. Christ, do you never stop to ask yourself, "What is the point?"'

'Yes I do,' John shouted back. 'We have a responsibility to do our best for our patients. The parents' decision was emotionally driven; they must've been exhausted, not in a position to decide. We still didn't know what his quality of his life would be, how much he might have improved. His breathing capacity might have increased over the next few days. Christ, Marcus, it was too early… a decision like that…'

Marcus turned and walked away.

He drove back to his own house instead of the rented room he'd existed in since Carole booted him out. He could hardly keep his eyes open, but he did. John's words echoing round and round his head: *quality of life.*

He knew Carole would be at her keep fit class. He opened the garage door, drove in, shut it again. He reached up for the hose, hanging on the hook where it always was. He uncoiled it, put one end on the exhaust pipe and one into the driver's seat. He wound the window back up and made himself comfortable.

It was the only decision he'd been sure of in a long time.

the man

Carl saw flies swarm and circle above him before he clouded over and passed out.

The man stood above Carl casting a long shadow. He scanned the ravine to check no one had seen him, and, sprinting to his car, he skidded away.

The man stood under a hot, powerful shower for a long time. He let the day sluice over him. He looked at his hands – they were still trembling. He walked from the en-suite to the bedroom. Jessica was propped up in bed, reading. 'Don't forget David and Carrie are coming for supper tomorrow.' She looked at him. 'You look tired. You should get some sleep.'

He slid in next to her between their satin sheets. He listened to her breathing settle and watched the laughing moon through the curtains. An hour later, he crept out of bed and was on the road. He drove carefully this time. He'd memorised the spot by landmarks. There were four big trees on the left, after the give-way sign, and two on the right. The body was lying in a gulley, hidden from view to the few cars that passed along the cliff. Only madmen and serious mountaineers climbed up there.

He shone his torch and spot-lit the still, crooked form below. He carefully clambered down the mountain ridge for as far as he could and peered over. *Please let him be dead.*

A red eye opened and shut slowly.

'Shit.' The man jumped back, scrambling up the crevice on all fours.

Carl moved his head to the left. He'd heard the car coming. He saw the man's silhouette outlined against a purple night sky. He'd rasped, 'Wait, please wait.' He'd listened to the man's running footsteps fade. 'Please, don't leave me. Help me.'

The car door slammed, the engine roared and gravel spat.

Tears streamed down Carl's face. The irony of being stranded alone in the Highlands wasn't lost on him. It was exactly what he'd wanted when he set out. He'd recently split with his fiancée and was thinking of moving abroad to get a fresh start. He'd told his flatmates, 'I need to get my head together. I'm going walking for the weekend. I'll book into a hostel on the way.'

No one would be looking for him. No one would wonder where he was. Carl was completely alone.

The man drove fast and slapped the wheel. 'What moron would be dawdling on a blind bend in the middle of the mountains?' He'd barely brushed him – but it was enough. It was a matter of inches, a matter of seconds, a domino effect; Time, Place, Action – and there was no replay. The walker had landed on a small outcrop a few metres below the bend in the road. If he'd rolled a few inches, he'd have plummeted off the cliff, but the young guy didn't look as if he could move. The man sniffed hard. 'It won't be long.' He thought of the torso twisted at an odd angle. 'He's a goner.'

The man threw his keys on the side and went straight to the drinks cabinet. He poured whisky and drank quickly. He poured more and drank again. He looked in the mirror, searching his eyes for telltale signs.

The following day was the dinner party.

'Are you ready yet?' Jessica shouted upstairs. 'They'll be here in a minute.'

'Yeah, I'm on my way.' He glugged the last of his wine and wiped his mouth with the back of his hand.

Carl stared out at a big, black sky. He tried to push off the blanket of hopelessness that was smothering him. He thought about locked-in syndrome. He'd read about it; people unable to move, complete paralysis. *At least I can move my arms, I can talk, I can piss.* He'd felt its warmth dribbling down his legs. He could feel his legs, but couldn't move them. He thought about death and dying. He'd read somewhere that unconscious people have heightened senses, that they can smell and hear acutely. He'd smelt the man. He'd smelt of wine and strong aftershave.

The doorbell rang, Jessica went to answer it. As he came down the stairs she hissed to him, 'At least make an effort to be sociable.'

He let the conversation wash over him, he smiled and poured wine and ate the food he couldn't really taste. He thought about that red eye opening slowly. Even if he had to wait until he died of dehydration, it wouldn't be long, not with those injuries. His father's words echoed: *You have to make a decision and stick to it.* He rubbed his finger around his glass. *Even if it's the wrong one, you live with it.* He thought briefly about ringing the police – but couldn't risk it. They'd be able to trace his mobile. He was well known locally; if he went to a public phone, someone would recognise him. Village eyes were everywhere.

'You're very quiet tonight,' Carrie smiled. 'Penny for your thoughts?'

'Sorry.' He rubbed his forehead.

'Right, who's for dessert?' Jessica clapped her hands. She liked her dinner parties to be light and fun.

Carl thought a lot about the man. He imagined him eating and drinking, living his day-in, day-out life, knowing all the time that another human being was out in the wilderness slowly dying. What sort of man would do that? Would he have told anyone? He might even have bragged about it. Carl felt a rush of anger scorch through his body. 'I'll get out of this shithole. I'll survive and I'll get my revenge on you.' He'd read about a man who got his arm trapped under a boulder in America. The man hacked his own arm off after five days, and he survived. 'Ha! This is nothing, I'm only day two.'

He looked up at the sky. He nostalgically thought of childhood camping and stargazing with his dad. He wondered whether people would think it was suicide, if he died. His flatmates knew he was cut up about Sarah leaving him, but he'd never top himself. Life was worth living, even the shitty bits. He clenched his fists. 'I won't let the bastard get away with it.' Carl ground his teeth. 'This is only day two. It's going to take more than this to kill me.'

The man's head throbbed. He hadn't slept again. He got up as the sun was rising on the pretence of going for a jog. He drove without music on. He parked the car further away this time and began to walk up. It was a beautiful view from up there. His life was good, he was a pillar of the community. He couldn't jeopardise everything for a tramp wandering aimlessly in the wild.

Carl heard an engine, his heart leapt. *The man's coming back. He's going to rescue me.* The noise drew nearer, slowly, labouring up the hill. It was a big vehicle; it sounded like a diesel, not the car, not the man's car. It stopped above him. Carl could hear it reversing, coming nearer to the edge.

'Go on a few more feet.'

It wasn't the man's voice. Carl suddenly felt panicky. He tried to swallow, but his dry tongue was too big. *What if the man has sent men to finish me off?*

'Right, help me heave the bugger over.'

Carl held his breath, his heart hammering. He heard grunting, and scraping.

'Bleedin' hell, it weighs a ton.'

'What d'you expect? It's a bloody cow. We'd have none of this carry-on if it hadn't been for Margaret Thatcher. She's the one that insisted farmers have to cough up to have dead livestock hoyed away. It's her fault there's rotting animals all over the country.' They grunted and the dead cow hurtled past Carl. He heard it thud against the rocks.

He heard hands clapping. 'Sorted.'

'Please help me.'

'What the hell? Did you hear summat?'

'No.'

'Listen.'

'Help me.'

'Bugger me – yes I did.'

'Jesus Christ! There's someone down there.'

They peered over. 'He's on a ledge, look.'

'What we gonna do?'

'If we pull him up, which I don't think we could, it's too bloody dangerous, they'll know we dumped the cow.'

'We can't leave the poor bugger.'

Carl heard the engine start up, the vehicle reversing, the engine fading down the mountainside.

'No, wait. Don't go. Please, help me.'

The man saw the lorry reversing as he came round the bend. He pressed himself against the cliff edge. The lorry drove down the steep incline away from him. He waited until the labouring engine was far down the mountainside. He chewed his lip. *He must've been rescued. Could they trace him to me?* There was the tiniest of dints on the bumper but the bodywork of his car had no marks, and he'd had it washed since. The tramp would never be able to identify him, it had all happened so quickly. The bastard would live, but now it had nothing to do with him. The man put his hands on his knees, taking deep breaths of relief.

Carl heard the sirens half an hour later. They took a while to find the exact spot from the anonymous garbled message, but eventually the torch was flashing over him.

'Over here, he's here. There's someone alive.'

'We'll get you patched up, pal,' said the ambulance man. 'Your legs are in a mess but the surgical team is on standby. We've got the best trauma team in the country.' He grinned cheerfully. 'Keeps us in business, eh?'

'I didn't fall, I was hit. A car hit me.'

'What? And it didn't stop?'

'No, and he came back to see if I'd died.'

'Bastard,' the ambulance man muttered under his breath.

'All this time he's known I was there.'

'How do you know it was a he?'

'I could smell his aftershave, and heard his voice.'

The ambulance man radioed the police. 'He claims he was knocked off the edge by a car. We're looking for a hit-and-run.' He turned to Carl. 'Can you describe him?'

'I didn't see him, just an outline.'

The ambulance man smacked his lips. 'We'll get him.'

At the hospital, a nurse smiled and leaned over the trolley. 'What's your name?'

'Carl.'

'Okay, Carl, we're going take you straight to theatre to get those legs fixed. Then we'll be carrying out more tests to check you're okay.'

'Thanks.'

'Thirty-two-year-old male, unclear history, but fell off the mountain sometime in the last three days. Is dehydrated, has multiple abrasions, and two broken legs, possible head injury, concussion with confusion.'

The anaesthetist patted his shoulder. 'I'll give you a relaxant and then a knock-out drug. By the time you count to ten you'll be asleep.'

Another figure entered the theatre, a silhouette against the bright theatre lights.

Carl grabbed the anaesthetist's hand. 'Wait!' He could smell strong aftershave, the voice was familiar.

The man spoke with authority. 'Intubate him quickly. He's delirious. The sooner we operate the better.'

Carl bucked and screamed. They pinned him down. The anaesthetist inserted a needle. Within seconds, Carl's limbs flopped and eyes shut.

Behind his mask, the man smiled. 'The state he's in, there's a high chance he'll have brain damage.' He held his scalpel carefully and cut deep.

bad blood

Paul loved summer storms. It was something different. Christmas, Easter and birthdays were just another day, but this was exciting; he might die and it wouldn't be his fault. He put his head back to feel the rain bite, splintering darts. A sudden flash of lightning forked. He counted 'one, two, three' before the crack of thunder. 'Only three miles and it's coming this way.' He opened his mouth, swallowing rain. He jogged to a tree split in two at the bottom of the park. It had been hit by lightning years ago. 'Now that's a thing I'd like to have seen.'

Paul thought it was alright to talk to himself in the middle of a storm, when there was no one around. 'Yes, by golly, a tree ripped apart. I wonder, did it look raw inside?' Another flash of lightning lit the sky. Paul spun round and round. He threw his head back. 'Come on, come and get me.'

Jack and Ryan ran into the newsagents for shelter. The rain pummelled the window, the sky dark. They watched fat raindrops bounce on the street.

Mr Turner, the newsagent, said, 'What d 'you want, lads? This isn't a bus shelter, you have to buy something.'

'Wanker,' hissed Jack.

'Well?' said Mr Turner.

'We're deciding what to buy,' said Ryan, pretending to look at the shelves. He wandered over to the rows of sweet jars and hummed.

'Well?' Mr Turner raised his eyebrow. 'What'll it be?'

'Have you got any "Uncle Joe's Mintballs"?'

'No.'

Ryan shook his head and wiped his nose. 'That's a shame.' He glanced outside, it was still bucketing.

'You two, you're wasting my time as usual. Go on, bugger off.'

'Can we stay until it eases off?'

Mr Turner's neck veins bulged. 'The bus stop's just there.' He opened the door. He knew those two were shoplifting but he could never catch them. 'Don't come back loitering in here again,' he barked. 'In fact, I'm banning you two, you're nothing but trouble.'

They ran off, grabbing a Kit Kat each and waving V-signs over their shoulders.

They lit up and huddled at the bus stop. 'Miserable git,' muttered Ryan.

'Eh look, there's Weirdo.' Jack pointed to a figure splashing in puddles.

'Nutter. With a bit of luck he'll get zapped by lightning.'

The storm evaporated. Sun shafts broke through silver clouds. The park glistened green and shiny. Paul was soaked through, and squelched as he walked. 'Cleansed,' he said, nodding, 'I feel cleansed.' He gazed across the horizon. 'Thank you, God.'

He saw them coming towards him, and walked quicker.

'Hey screwball, first shower of the year, eh?'

Paul put his head down and tried to walk faster. They followed him, taunting. 'When they going to put you back inside, eh?'

'Let's hope they throw the key away next time.'

'Fruitcakes should be kept locked in a tin.' Ryan spat at Paul's feet.

Paul's lips moved but he kept the words zipped inside. He veered, walking fast to the shop for safety.

'Morning, Paul,' said Mr Turner. 'Quite a storm, eh? Looks like you got caught in it.'

'It was, yes, I certainly did.'

'Mind you don't drip on my papers. What can I get for you?'

'Just the milk today, please.' Paul bought milk daily. He didn't have a fridge, he didn't want a fridge, they hummed too much.

He went back to his flat and listened to the radio. Today, he had his appointment at the doctor's. It would be two conversations with two other people in one day. Like buses, they all come at once.

Dr Stone was running late and Mrs Todd refused to be hurried.

'I can't explain the pain exactly. It balloons out from under my ribs and goes across my belly button,' she said, grimacing.

'Does anything make it worse?'

'Not really, I'm not sure...'

'How often do you get it?'

'Pardon?'

'I said how often do you get the pain...?'

Dr Stone checked his list while she droned on. Paul was next – good, he could hurry him along.

A receptionist spread her holiday photos out behind the desk, 'Oh, I look so fat in that one.'

'No, you don't,' said the other receptionist.

'Oh, I do.'

Paul waited. The man behind Paul coughed and she looked up, pursing her lips. 'Just take a seat in the waiting room.'

Paul sat and watched the screen carefully. It came up with your name so you knew when the doctor was ready to see you. Sometimes it came up with other messages, but he ignored them.

'Sit down, Paul. How are you?' Dr Stone kept his eyes on his computer screen. He checked to see who was in next after Paul. *Jean Withers. Christ, what a day.* He nodded while Paul said he felt well. 'Except those boys call me names. Why do they do that?'

'What boys, Paul?' He glanced up.

'The ones I've told you about every time I come. They live nearby and for some reason say bad things to me.'

'Some kids are obnoxious, they're bullies.'

'Do they ever shout at you? Why do they pick on me?' asked Paul.

'Er no, well yes, not those kids, but different ones maybe, sometimes. Teenagers can be very anti-social.' He looked at Paul – he was a mountain of a man. His trousers hung half-mast, and his belly strained against a stripy T-shirt. Paul liked stripes. His fuzzy hair bushed out as if he'd been electrocuted.

'Have you ever thought of getting a haircut, Paul?'

'Pardon?'

'Your hair is quite long. Kids notice differentness. They might not bother you if you were less... if your hair was shorter.'

'So if I have my hair cut, they might leave me alone?'

'Maybe. I'm glad everything is stable, Paul. I'll see you next month.' Dr Stone got up and opened the door.

Paul went to the convenience shop. He looked at the offers. 'A pair of scissors, please.'

'You're in luck, Paul, they're on offer.'

'I know, I can see.'

Mr Turner smiled. 'I wish everyone was as straight-forward as you, Paul, always keen for a bargain.'

Paul nodded, he wasn't sure if thank you was the right thing to say, so said nothing.

Two weeks later, he saw the nurse for his injection.

'Hi Paul, you look well.'

'I've had my hair cut.'

She smiled. 'I can see. Did you do it yourself?'

'Yes, I did, I jolly well did.' Paul had practised this reply. He thought she might ask him as he'd cut his hair very short. He looked different. He'd heard posh people on the radio say 'jolly' – it sounded like tasting jelly.

'Those boys are still calling me names, even with my hair cut.'

'Kids, who'd have them, eh?'

'I don't know, but people do.' Paul didn't know what she meant at all. 'Do you have them?'

She laughed. 'Yes, I do.'

'I don't understand why they're so–'

She looked at her watch. 'Let's check your blood pressure, eh?' she interrupted.

Paul knew he had to be quiet while she listened.

'Well, that's fine so we can get on and give you your injection.' She drew the curtains round him and he dropped his pants. She jabbed the needle.

'Why do you think they do it?' he asked, hitching his trousers back up.

'I'll see you in a month, Paul,' she said.

The receptionists were still laughing as he left.

Paul walked up the stairs to his flat; he never took the lift. He hated being trapped and the feeling of being watched. He heard voices as he put his key in the door – he always left the radio on.

He had cereal for tea like usual, with tinned fruit because a man on the radio had said fruit stops you getting cancer. It was mandarin bits.

On the radio he heard there'd been a spate of knifings in London – gang warfare. 'I'm very glad I don't live in London, very glad indeed,' nodded Paul, tipping his bowl to drink the mandarin juice.

Ryan and Jack skived school again. They hung around the kiddie park, sitting on the swings. 'I'm bored,' sniffed Jack.

'But if we go into town, someone might report us like last time,' said Ryan.

'Look, it's crackerjack.'

Paul was heading for the shop. 'I wonder what would happen if there was a tsunami here?' he asked himself. 'After all, Britain is an island surrounded by water, and Iceland's not far away and earthquakes could be shaking the ocean bed and could send giant waves our way.' Paul had heard about tsunamis and earthquake activity on the radio. 'I wonder if one day the earth will split in two, and would it be across or lengthways?' He nodded. 'I expect it would depend on how strong, and where the earthquake or volcano was.'

Ryan nudged Jack. 'Come on, let's see if we can get him to fetch us some fags. Turner won't sell us nowt.'

They ran round the bus stop and leapt out in front of Paul. He nearly jumped out of his skin.

'Hey nuthead, what you up to?' They blocked his path.

'I beg your pardon?' Paul felt a rush of heat burn up his neck.

'Do you wanna join our gang?' sniggered Jack.

'No, I don't believe gangs are a good thing.'

'Our gang is. We'd be like the three musketeers. In't that right, Ryan?'

'Yeah, we'd be the good guys,' Ryan nodded. 'Are you going to the shop?'

Paul blinked. 'Yes, I am.' He wanted to run.

'Will you get us some fags?'

Paul blinked again. 'Yes, I will.' He rocked from one foot to the other. They emptied their pockets and gave him seventy-two pence.

Paul clenched his hands, not sure what to do next.

'Bring them back here,' said Jack. 'Then you'll be one of the gang.'

'A brotherhood,' sniggered Ryan.

Paul counted the money shakily outside the shop. He muttered, 'I don't want to be in a gang or brotherhood, they misunderstand me.' His fingers were clothes pegs. 'The man on the radio said gangs need to be stamped out.'

Mr Turner frowned. 'I didn't know you smoked, Paul?'

'I don't, Mr Turner. This is in case I decide I want to.'

Mr Turner laughed. 'You are a card, Paul.'

'How many cigarettes will this buy?' He held out his money.

'Make it up to a pound and you can have six, Paul.' Mr Turner opened a packet and popped the cigarettes in a bag. He was fond of Paul and his funny ways. 'What about your milk?'

'I don't need it today, thank you, Mr Turner.'

Mr Turner frowned. *Strange.*

Paul's hands were sweating as he carried the cigarettes out.

'Ta, mate.' Ryan and Jack took three each. They high-fived and laughed. 'To the Brotherhood.'

Paul stuttered, 'I d-d-d-don't want to be in a gang.'

Jack put his face close up to Paul's. 'Fuck off back to the loony-bin then.' He pushed him backwards.

The receptionist who was very orange from her holiday was cross with Paul. 'How important is it, Paul? Is it an emergency?'

'Yes, it is, it most certainly is.' He bit the inside of his lip hard.

The receptionist clicked her tongue loudly.

Dr Stone was surprised. 'Bit early for your monthly check-up, Paul?'

'It's an emergency.' Paul shifted from one foot to the other, his hair sticking up in clumps of bum fluff. He'd run all the way from the park to the surgery. His heart hadn't pounded like this in a long time. He clenched and unclenched his fists.

'What is it, Paul?'

'I'm concerned gang warfare is coming up from London.'

'What?'

'It's called Brotherhood.'

Dr Stone smothered a smile. 'We don't have the demographic profile for gang warfare in Summerdale.' He pushed his biro up and down. 'By that, I mean we don't have lots of gangs here.'

'Not yet, but they're recruiting.'

'I don't think so, Paul.'

'I've heard about it on the radio.'

'Ahh well, maybe you shouldn't listen to the radio quite so much.'

Paul rubbed his head. 'I don't know what to do. They might have knives.'

'Probably not,' sighed Dr Stone, looking at his watch.

'And I'm worried about tsunamis, too.'

Dr Stone raised an eyebrow. 'Did you have your last injection, Paul?'

'I certainly did.'

Dr Stone looked at his list of patients for the afternoon; he didn't have all day. 'Paul, when you come in for your next monthly appointment we'll have a good chat about this. These appointments today are for emergencies, this isn't really an emergency.'

'But what about the gangs?'

'You're a big lad, you can look after yourself. Don't let them bully you.'

'I don't like gangs,' he said to himself going home, 'not at all.'

Paul sat on his single bed staring at the wall. He stroked his candlewick bedspread. It was neat and straight, he did it nice every day. He looked round the room. There was a mirror on top of the chest of drawers. Next to it was the radio, a comb and his new scissors. He got up and turned the radio off like Dr Stone told him to.

'I'll have to take his advice and fend for myself.' He felt hot and sweaty and not well at all, but knew the receptionist wouldn't give him another appointment.

He held on tight to his candlewick bedspread as if clinging to a lifeboat. He scrunched it up into a knot and bit his fist. 'Oh dear, I don't want gangs.' He stood and looked in the mirror. 'You need to take care of yourself, Paul.' He took a deep breath, reached for the scissors, and set out to face the Brotherhood.

the feeling

Vince lay awake staring at the net curtains. After a while, the patterns looked like plucked eye sockets. He got up and brought Linda a cup of tea in bed. He gently shook her awake. 'I've a meeting in London and have to get the early train.'

Blearily, she sat up. 'Thanks for the tea.' She put her hand on his arm. 'Vince, I know this isn't the time, but we need to talk.'

'I've got to go, today's important.' He brushed her cheek. 'I'm sorry.'

'Good luck,' she muttered. The door was already closed.

Later that day, Vince grabbed a coffee at King's Cross for the journey home; it was thin and frothy, like sucking on wet cotton wool. He wiped the moustache it left on his upper lip and stared out the window. The train was almost full, and as the whistle blew, a bloke in a too small pin-striped suit slumped heavily in the seat next to him, knocking Vince's arm off the rest. The man was on the phone. 'Just got it.' He wiped a greasy sheen off his face. 'Yeah right, laters.' He smelt of meat and a sweat rash spread out above his shirt collar.

The man took off his jacket. There were big, wet patches under his arms. He stretched over Vince to put his jacket in the overhead rack, his crotch at nose level. Vince turned away. The man sat splay-legged, rummaging in his briefcase. He pulled out a Big Mac. He ate as if someone might snatch it, as if he hadn't eaten for days: bite, swallow; bite, swallow; mouth open, chomping. He cleared the lot, crumpled the paper and leant back burping.

Vince blankly looked at his reflection in the window. He could see new wrinkles and deep frown lines.

The bloke shifted in his seat; it smelt as if he'd farted.

Vince's phone rang.

'Hi, are you on the train?' asked Linda.

'Yeah, it's busy.'

'I thought maybe this might be a good time to talk. I've taken the kids over to Mum's.'

'I'm not sure.' He hesitated. 'I'm sorry, I don't know why...'

'Vince, what is it about death that scares you so much? You've woken me every night this week with these night terrors. I'm trying to understand.'

They'd met fifteen years ago. She remembered swapping childhoods – schools, friends, family highs and lows. He'd told her he'd gone through a funny phase of being terrified of death. He couldn't be specific about what had frightened him – *the blackness* he'd called it, before changing the subject. That was a long time ago but now *the blackness* was smothering him again.

'It's more of a feeling,' he said quietly. He rubbed his forehead. 'I'm sorry. I don't know why this has come back.' He dropped his voice to a whisper. 'It's completely irrational.'

'Is everything okay at work?'

'Linda,' he said firmly, 'there's nothing I'm hiding from you.'

'I can't function if I don't get some decent sleep soon,' she said wearily.

Vince pinched the bridge of his nose. 'I wish there was a reason, but there isn't.'

'Are you having dark thoughts?' she asked slowly.

'What do you mean?'

'Self harm?'

'Linda, I've told you, there's nothing I'm hiding from you.' He glanced at the fat bloke. 'We'll talk when I'm home.'

Vince analysed the day's meeting. He'd done nothing wrong, but hadn't shined either. That's what the company expected now; it was getting harder.

Linda collected the kids and tucked them up in bed. An hour later, Tom came downstairs for the third time since he'd gone to bed.

'What now?'

'David says his daddy has gone to live in another house. Will you and Daddy always live in our house?'

'I hope so.'

'Cross your heart and hope to die.'

'No, I can't do that, Tom.'

'Why?'

'Because sometimes mummies and daddies fall out.'

'But you and Daddy won't?'

'I hope we won't, but I can't promise.' She picked at a mark on the table.

Tom's eyes widened. 'What will happen if you fall out of love with me?'

'Darling, I would never fall out of love with you.' She hugged him tight.

'But why would you fall out with Daddy?'

'Sometimes grown-ups... oh, never mind. It's way past your bedtime.' She led him upstairs and kissed his forehead as she tucked him in. 'Night, night. Sleep well.'

'Tell Daddy to come up when he comes in.'

'I will.'

The snack trolley trundled down the aisle. The bloke rummaged in his pocket. Vince sighed heavily. *What a crap day.*

'Bad day?' the bloke asked.

'Not great,' Vince replied, nodding.

'Here, let me buy you a drink.' Ignoring Vince's protestations, he ordered. 'Six cans of lager and a quart of whisky, please.'

He nudged Vince. 'Nothing a few drinks can't sort out, eh? Cheers.'

'Er, thanks.' Vince drank; it was cold and sharp. He drank again.

'There's some good football on this weekend,' the bloke said.

'Yes, Arsenal v Chelsea should be good.'

They drifted into football talk; drink, talk, drink again.

'Sounds like you were getting it in the ear there, mate?'

'No, it's just…' He shrugged. 'I don't know. Are you married?'

'Nah, love 'em and leave 'em, that's my motto. Once you get serious, all women want is to talk.'

Vince nodded and took another drink.

The train was held up at York. The bloke insisted Vince should have a whisky chaser. 'Keep me company, eh? Cheers.'

When they eventually drew into Vince's station, his head was spinning. He stood unsteadily. 'Right, well, er, see you around.'

'Cheers, and you have a good evening,' the bloke said, smirking.

Linda sat tensely on the edge of the settee, waiting.

Vince opened the front door quietly. His face dropped.

She rankled. 'Oh Vince, don't look so disappointed to see me.'

'Linda, please don't.'

She patted the settee. 'Come and sit down, talk to me.'

'Let me take my jacket off first. And I really need to eat.' He stubbed his toe on the armchair by the door, almost losing his balance. 'Shit.'

Linda's eyes narrowed. 'Have you been drinking, Vince? That's why you're so late.' She thumped the cushion next to her. 'I don't know why I bother.'

Tom appeared at the bottom of the stairs.

'Tom, what did I tell you?' she snapped. 'Go back to bed now.'

Tom's lip wobbled.

'I'll sort him out,' said Vince. He swept Tom up into his arms, 'Come on, buster.' He carried him to his bed and gently tucked him in.

Tom looked up at him. 'Dad...?' His eyes were dark pools.

'Yes, son.'

'If you and Mummy fall out of love, you'll have to live on your own, or with a new lady. David's daddy's got a new lady, but David doesn't like her – she smells funny.'

'Well, there's no new lady, and I love Mummy lots so that's not going to happen.'

Tom hugged his neck. 'Good, because Mummy said she might not live in the same house as you forever. That won't happen will it, Daddy?'

Vince felt kicked in the belly. His voice husky, he said, 'That's silly talk, we'll always be together.'

'She said she couldn't promise.'

'Don't worry, son, everything will be fine. Night, night. Sleep well.'

'I will.'

Vince grabbed the banister. He couldn't breathe. Later, while Linda was in the bath he rummaged her knickers out of the linen basket and sniffed them for another man.

Linda shook Vince awake. 'Shh, it's only a dream.' She rubbed her gummy eyes. Vince had woken screaming again.

He blinked, wide-eyed. 'Oh, God.' He dropped his head in his hands and shook slowly side to side. 'I don't know what it is, but it's interfering with my work, with us, with everything.' He reached for her. 'I'm sorry.' His hand was trembling.

'Would you consider seeing a counsellor?'

'No. It'll pass. It did when I was a kid, and it will again.'

At work, he googled *sixth sense* and *premonitions*. It threw up a load of hocus-pocus twaddle. His head pounded – a hangover and lack of sleep. He clenched his fists.

He went for a walk at lunchtime. Nausea had killed his appetite. It was a crisp, autumnal day, the sun shining between dancing leaves. He walked briskly, with a purpose, head clearing.

He was at the entrance to the park when he saw the dead rabbit, its bulging eyes caught in the moment of death. A gust of wind scuttled leaves and dust over the dead body. The feeling hit him like a sledgehammer. It overwhelmed, his whole body was bathed in sweat, his heart raced. He thought he'd die there and then. He stumbled, staggering backwards, and unsteadily threw himself deep into the park trees, hiding like a wild animal.

Half an hour later, he scraped himself into a semblance of order, and brushing his suit down he walked slowly out of the park. He waited at the pedestrian crossing, the traffic roared. It was too near, he was too near. Within seconds, with one step – he could be dead. He held knuckle-white onto the lamppost. The feeling taunted him; he didn't trust himself not to stumble.

The green man flashed. People barged ahead, a man behind barked, 'You gonna move or stand there all day, mate?' The man side-stepped round Vince and strode across the road. Vince tried to peel himself from the post to follow him, but his fingers clenched tighter. He lost sight of the man, and knew he'd never make it across the road.

Vince gasped as if he was diving into water, eyes closed tight. He wiped his forehead with a hankie and after a moment, peeled his hand from the lamppost and went back into the park. He found a quiet bench tucked away and wept.

Vince stayed on the bench, watching the leaves blow around. A rabbit hopped across the path. The dead one was so easily forgotten. No one was indispensible.

The autumn colours were mesmerising, like a living fire, yet all in stages of decay. Within a couple of weeks they'd be gone. It was the finality, the black hole that made him shudder and shake. He rubbed his hands down his trousers and texted his secretary: *Something has cropped up – cancel this afternoon.*

He craved somewhere dark and cool. He'd gone to church with his family as a boy; it had bored him. As a teenager, he voted with his feet and opted out.

He went to the nearest church. It was old and it took a while for his eyes to get accustomed to the dark. Incense wafted like cobwebs settling on him. A row of candles flickered at a small side alter. He walked up the aisle slowly, his shoes sounding very loud.

All around was death. It watched him from the stained glass windows, the crypts, the body of Christ, the bloody breast of the Sacred Heart, the martyred saints. Vince scraped his hands down his face as if it was melting wax.

With time, the calm dark crept under his skin. He stayed all afternoon, trying to look death in the face.

When the priest silently appeared at his side, it made him jump.

'I'm sorry if I startled you,' the priest said, 'I need to lock up the church.' He offered Vince a pitiful smile.

'Yes, of course, I'll go.' Vince nodded, embarrassed.

'We open in the morning at eight for nine o'clock Mass.'

'Thank you.'

Vince stood on the church steps and texted Linda: *Late meeting, don't wait for me to have tea.*

He dithered on the church steps. He wished he could have stayed in the church, surrounded by death – it had soothed him. He shivered and began walking.

The gate creaked. The cemetery behind the church wasn't a well-kept one; most of the graves were very old and overgrown with lichen and moss. He stopped at each grave to read the inscriptions. Lots of them were dead before his age. He could see no sense or reason as to why they died. There was no pattern. He didn't know why he was fighting it so hard. It was a battle he could never win. He was tired, the night was drawing in. He lay against the cold stone. He liked the smell of earth. He closed his eyes. It grew colder and darker.

david's journey

David carried a coffee back to his table. Mary would've had a pastry. She'd have cut him a corner and said, 'Go on, have a taste.' He never bothered to buy one for himself.

He looked at the departures. Two hours to kill. Mary would've taken him round the shops, browsed in the duty free and tried perfumes on. He stared at the flights screen; it seemed as if time was standing still.

He was nervous. This was his first trip alone in thirty-five years. The kids urged him to do it. 'You're doing so well, Dad.'

'Am I?'

He'd joined a bridge club and became involved in parish activities. He'd read the papers back to front, even the ads. He'd water the garden, listen to Radio Four, chat to the newsagent and meander down Sainsbury's aisles. The kids bought him a bread machine. A pinch of this or a shake of that could make all the difference. He could pass a whole morning agreeably tinkering tastes. Proper cooking he hadn't got into. It somehow seemed so futile cooking for one. He kept body and soul together with microwave meals, although he needed two to fill him up. It was a ritual to be got through. He usually ate out of the plastic container; it saved on washing up.

The kids had a little rota, they took it in turns to have him round. They thought they sounded spur-of-the-moment. 'We're having a barbeque, Dad, why don't you come?'

He appreciated the thought.

It was a long winter. He didn't go out unless he had to, the roads were treacherous. He became quite an addict to morning TV, and wouldn't miss *Countdown* or *Pointless.* Mrs Joyce came once a week to clean. He resented her singing – it was too cheerful.

Often he looked out the window across the fields to rolling hills. It was one of the reasons they'd bought the house. She became ill six months after he retired. There was nothing they could do.

The kids suggested, 'How about a holiday?'

He balked at the idea of going with them. They liked camping.

'Why not go alone?' said Peter, his eldest. 'There are lots of holidays for singles.'

Singles sounded young and fun. He was widowed, sad and lonely.

The kids persisted. 'No harm in looking at what's on offer.'

Even looking across the fields to the hills seemed daunting some days.

He'd always fancied Canada. He needed something to look forward to. He had plenty of money and maybe by next year he'd be too old.

'You could go on an organised trip, Dad. You'll meet some nice people.'

He'd briefly joined a choir, but other people seemed to irritate him – too bossy, too nosy or too chatty. He knew it was his fault.

'Toronto, I'm going to go to Toronto.'

'Great, Dad, that's great.'

'I'm travelling alone, that way I can pick and choose who I chat to.'

'Wouldn't you be better going in a group? Sometimes it can seem odd when strangers come up and talk,' Joanne said.

He noticed she wrinkled her nose in exactly the same way as Mary.

'I'll go on daytrips, it'll be fine.'

At the airport he wasn't so sure. Everyone seemed to have someone. Even the business people had their phones to talk to.

The hotel was central, a lovely room and good service. He'd read up about Toronto, fifty-two per cent of the population isn't Canadian. It was a hotchpotch of multi-nationals. He liked that – if no one belonged, everyone belonged. He wasn't good at small talk but they were.

'From Northumberland? I've heard it's beautiful,' a young waitress said.

'Yes, I suppose it is.'

The hotel arranged trips to Niagara Falls. He booked himself onto one and fell into talking with an American couple staying at the same hotel. She was a psychotherapist, he was a psychiatrist. They were very intense. They worried about his bereavement, they *understood* how he felt. He wanted to punch them.

On the return coach he sat next to a sulky teenager to avoid further analysis. The kid leaned against the window with his iPod plugged in. He was spotty and chewed gum. Occasionally, with the sway of the bus, they brushed arms. It was comforting to feel warm skin.

Part of the attraction of Toronto was a buzzing literary scene. Benson Davis was giving a reading with a questions and answers session. He was one of David's favourite writers. Seven thirty at the Henry Club.

David asked at the hotel desk, 'Can you tell me where this is?'

'Yeah, sure.' She got a map and pointed out the Henry Club. 'It's here, behind the university.'

He went upstairs to ring Joanne. 'Yes, I'm having a good time. Niagara Falls was a bit disappointing, but the rest is good: nice hotel, lots of places to eat. I'm going to a reading of Benson Davis tonight. I'll try and get a signed copy for you.'

'Great, Dad, thank you. And Dad…'

'Yes?'

'I'm proud of you.'

His eyes prickled. He cleared his throat. 'I'd better get going.'

He decided to walk, the university was easy to find. It was a beautiful evening; people strolled, relaxed and laughing. They smiled at him, he smiled back. He was surprised – *it is good to be alive.*

He walked up the street twice; he checked both sides. Eventually he popped into a café. 'Could you tell me where the Henry Club is, please?'

'Sure,' said a man with a ponytail and a ring through his lip. 'You go down to Chinatown, and get onto Dundale Street. It's just there.' He pointed to a map.

'I was told it was here?'

'It moved six months ago.'

'How far away is Chinatown?'

'An hour's walk, it's probably best to get a cab.'

David hated being late. If Benson Davis had started reading, they might not let him in. He hurried to the main road and flagged down a taxi. 'To Dundale Street, please. I'm in a rush.'

The taxi driver clicked his fare dial. He was small, maybe South American. He nodded, pulling away.

They moved bumper to bumper. 'Isn't there a quicker way?' David asked.

'This time of the evening is always busy.'

David glanced at his watch. 'Please hurry.'

The taxi driver nodded again. Suddenly he swung a sharp left into a dark, sweaty alley. He weaved through a vein of backstreets, knocking bags of rubbish. The buildings crowded in. David clutched his seat; something didn't feel right. They zigzagged through the maze. David felt a wave of panic. 'Where are you taking me?' he stuttered.

The taxi driver shouted over his shoulder. 'Dundale Street.'

David made a mental note of his name – *José* – and the taxi firm above the ticking fare dial.

'But it's in Chinatown, that's central, we're heading north.'

'This is longer but quicker because of the traffic.' He swerved to miss a stray cat.

David clutched his phone, he didn't know if the emergency services were 999. He didn't have his glasses; he couldn't see the numbers without them. He wiped his forehead. 'I'd like you to return to the main streets, please.' He spoke with as much authority as he could, but his voice squeaked. 'This seems a very long way round, it will be unnecessarily expensive.'

The taxi man sighed and took two more sharp lefts. In a few minutes, David saw a busy street ahead. He sagged with relief. They joined the traffic, a long snaking queue. They crawled.

If this had happened with Mary, she'd have laughed about it. She'd keep it as a funny story to tell the kids when they got home. 'Dad thought we were being kidnapped.' David looked at the taxi man in the mirror, their eyes met briefly. *He thinks I'm a stupid old man who doesn't know what he's doing. Someone he can take for a ride and charge a fortune.* His eyes watered, he blinked. *Get a grip, it's not the end of the world.* Sometimes, since Mary died, little things did seem like the end of the world. 'How long now?' he asked.

'A lot longer time in the traffic,' the taxi driver said, nodding his head. 'I could've got you there in fifteen minutes the other way, but you tourists, you're all the same.' His voice shook. 'You think I'm trying to rip you off, you think I take you the long way so I can charge more.' He glanced at David in the mirror. 'I'm not. All I'm trying to do is make a life for my wife and son.' He rubbed his forehead. 'That's all I'm trying to do.'

To David's horror, the man sobbed – a tired, weary sob, like a dog that has been kicked too many times.

They sat in silence hardly moving, the journey seemed to last forever. When they arrived at Dundale Street, the taxi driver pulled up at the Henry Club. He looked at the fare dial. 'That's twelve dollars.' He bleakly stared out his window and muttered in a monotone voice, 'I have never cheated anyone in my life. I am a decent human being.'

David handed him twenty dollars. 'Keep the change. I'm sorry…'

The taxi driver stared straight ahead. 'I'm sorry, too.' He pressed eight dollars change into David's palm and drove away.

David slipped into the back of the auditorium. Benson Davis had been delayed: 'Toronto traffic is terrible, sorry folks.' He began his reading just as David sat down.

The next day over breakfast David decided to go to the CNN tower. It was a tourist must. It was another sunny day. He slipped his glasses on and stepped out.

David queued at the CNN tower with a school trip of children. They were about thirteen years old, shrieking hormones. The boys jostled, the girls giggled. They raced round him, but he didn't mind. He read the information blurb: *the CNN tower; one of the tallest buildings in the world.* He stepped into the glass lift, a gaggle of kids squeezed in behind him. They whooshed upwards. The kids obligingly screamed as it hurtled skyward. At the top of the tower was an amazing view. The whole of Toronto stretched on and on for as far as he could see. He walked around the tower, the world beneath his feet. The kids all headed for the glass-floored area, pushing and shoving each other onto it. He went to the opposite side. It was quieter, only a few Japanese clicking cameras.

He stood and stared out at the tapestry below. *All those little lives woven into the mishmash of day-to-day existence.* It made him feel less lonely. David thought of the taxi driver somewhere out there. He probably lived on the cheaper outskirts. He'd have driven home last night after yet another bad day. David guiltily remembered the man's words: *I am a decent human being.* He looked out across the horizon. A beautiful, blue sky framed skyscrapers and towering buildings, but the taxi driver probably rarely got to see the sky.

David's stomach flipped as the lift dropped downwards. He stepped out and switched his phone on. He punched in the number. 'I'd like picking up from CNN tower please, and I'd like José, car 742.'

'Fifteen minutes wait for José,' a voice crackled.

'I'll wait.'

José pulled up and flickered recognition. He stared ahead and asked in a flat voice, 'Where to?'

'José, take me round your city, I know you know these streets well.' David smiled. 'I'd like you to give me a tour of all the sights. Tell me as much about them as you can.'

José raised his eyebrow.

David offered his hand. 'Please?'

José hesitantly reached out and they shook hands. He nodded, opening the car door for David, and they pulled away.

elephants on the beach

As a kid, you used to love cycling along the beach. The frothy sea chopped and slapped. If the tide was out, you'd cycle across the sand, free-wheeling. With a wild wind blowing and your legs whirling, there was nothing to stop you falling off the edge of the horizon.

One day, you turned onto the sand and nearly fell off your bike. *Are they a mirage?* You couldn't take your eyes off them – elephants on the beach, six of them trunk to tail, whooshing geysers. A man scrubbed them with a big brush. One trumpeted; you could tell they liked it. They paddled and swung their legs and tails, squirting and splashing, having fun. Their heaviness was lifted, like big, grey balloons set free. You hung around until the man marched them back in line. You shook your head, smiling. Thinking of them made you happy.

You wanted to see the elephants again, so went to Blackpool circus under the Tower, where they lived. They were kept in the dark, cooped up in small cages. Their dead eyes spoke of misery. They cowered, nudging the comfort of cold bars. You prayed the elephants could shut their eyes and remember, remember that day on the beach – the day when they were free.

Peering out your grimy window, you think about the elephants a lot. Everything in the city is grey, the sky and streets a pencil-scribbled mess. Winter is lasting forever, you long for sunshine, warmth and colour – you need something to look forward to. A clock ticks, you try to get back to your revision but the words bump and jump on the page. You pull your cardigan tight around your shoulders. The city damp gnaws your bones. You put your head on the desk and close your eyes. You let yourself drift.

You jumpstart awake with clanging bins being emptied outside. A fly slowly climbs up the grubby windowpane. You roll up a practice exam paper and splat it. The yellow goo stains the window, hanging snottily. You watch it drop. Flies are the most dangerous animals in the world, you know that. They carry germs, millions of germs. Poisons are floating in the air, up your nasal passages, down your throat, in your lungs, through your bloodstream. You can feel it happening, you're buzzing.

Your head pings a kaleidoscope of colours, miles of winking rainbows. It helps you see what's happening with the germs. They're a flickering wildfire running over brushwood that you can't see. No one can, but it's burning, catching the air, spreading, getting ready to kill.

You jump up out of your room, and slam the door to contain them. You need to act fast, to clean that room, disinfect and bleach it. You have to do it now. You grab your flatmate's coat and run out in slippers. You can't risk infection going back in that room. You hurry downstairs, wondering whether you'll be able to buy one of those masks they wear in epidemics. Would they be in a chemist or supermarket? You fall into a drizzling evening, shoving past people. All the time germs will be multiplying. You don't look at faces, there are too many eyes.

In the shops, the aisles are full of steamy people. Arms touch, you flinch away – you could infect them all. Someone holds your arm, you shake them off.

'Hey, slow down, it's me – Suzie.' A girl on your course stares. 'Are you okay?'

You pull away. 'Sorry, I'm in a hurry.'

Suzie runs alongside. 'Wait up, you look terrible.'

You push her. 'Piss off.'

You skid past perfume, hair products and cosmetics. You run to the nearest till, interrupting, 'Where's the bleach?'

A woman in the queue tuts loudly. The girl points you to the left aisle. You screech up and find the bleach at last. You grasp three bottles; you'll blast the place, annihilate the proliferation. There's a long queue at the till. You twitch, waiting. You fumble in your flatmate's coat pockets, not sure if there's any money. There's no time to waste. The spores will be multiplying, the room a death trap. You need to get back to stop the spread. You shift from one foot to another. An old woman at the front of the queue is trying to pay in change. She drops her coins. You can't wait any longer. You run. Someone shouts. You weave, hugging the bleach close, jogging fast.

You get in, throw the coat off, hold your breath. You go full frontal assault, bleaching all hard surfaces in your room. You squirt neat bleach on the window, watch it cut a trail through the infected minefield. You run out to breathe – deep breaths then run back in. You do this again and again, risking your life for others. Your hands burn and blister, you don't care. You only stop when you run out of bleach. You can't rest, body twitching. They might be still lurking, the killers.

Your flatmate, Dee, rolls home, drunk as usual. 'Christ, it smells like a chemical fall-out in here. What the hell happened?'

'I had to disinfect everywhere; we were covered in germs. It was disgusting. They were everywhere, flies, multiplying. God knows if we'll get through this.'

'Where are the flies now then?'

You tell her, 'I think I've got it under control. It spurted out, but–'

Dee interrupts. '*It?* There was *one* fly?'

'One fly, millions of germs, literally millions.'

'Oh Christ, you really are nuts.'

Dee goes into her room, where Den, her spotty boyfriend, is hovering. He taps the side of his head. 'Eggshell, could crack any minute.' He smirks and slams the door.

You go to your room and shiver, hands red raw. You lie under the covers, and hear other flies but never see them. They are increasingly conniving, perhaps a new species. You need to be vigilant.

In the morning, about 4.30am, you get up. You go for a jog. You feel so alive. Today is a God-given day. You know you're chosen for something special. When you get back, you're starving. You eat nearly a whole packet of muesli. When the milk runs out, you have it dry, handful after handful. You look at your books; you know it all. The formulae and calculi, they're in your head. You have theories, new theories not even dreamed of. You go out to see if there's anywhere open to buy milk, you're still hungry.

You jog again, a mean, lean running machine, running with the grace and beauty of an athlete through alleys and moonlit streets. A young lad staggers towards you, he's drunk. You think he's cute, and there's no one else around. You run up to him. 'Hi,' you say, licking your lips. The dark streets are deserted. 'Let's do it, here and now.' You're horny as hell. You stick your tits out. 'I said hi.'

'Huh? Do I know you?' He burps.

'No, but you could.' You pout, run your hand down the front of his shirt. It's damp. You like that – hot and sticky. You run your hand further down, rub his crotch.

He jumps back. 'Hey, what's going on?'

'Come on, big boy' – pulling his hand onto your breast – 'come on, let's fuck.'

'I can't, I'm too sick.' He leans against the wall to stop falling over. He smells of beer and puke, you don't care. You're desperate for some dick; you want shafting hard. You put your lips to his, open your mouth.

'I can't.' He pushes away, staggering. You want to hit him, want to screw him. You hear him throw up.

You leave and run again. You come to someone huddled in a doorway, he smells bad. His voice rasps and his fingers are brown with fags. He's rough, he thinks you're a dream and might pop and disappear. He shags you like dogs in the streets do; sixty seconds flat. After, you wonder what his name is.

Nowhere is open. There's a bottle of milk on a doorstep, you grab it and run home. The sky is blood red. It's a good sign for you.

Back at the flat, you gobble more muesli. You write a poem, then another, then another. Your mind is electric, alive. You begin to get theories down on paper, they're vitally important. You don't have time to go for your exams, there's too much to do. You have papers all over your room, and paintings. You're expressing theories in visual terms – they are masterpieces. You don't have time to sleep.

Interfering Suzie calls in the middle of your major discovery. 'I've been so worried about you,' she says.

'Why?' You try to keep the formulae in your head. You mustn't let them slip away.

'Can I come in?'

'No, I'm busy, I'm very busy.'

'Aren't you going to come in for your exam?'

'I'm too busy.' You try to shut the door.

'What are you working on?' asks Suzie, her foot in the door.

'Electricity.'

'Show me.'

You're bursting to tell someone, someone who'll recognise your brilliance. Suzie's not stupid; she's been getting firsts throughout the course. You show her how you can generate electricity yourself in your own body. You make palm sparks, showing Suzie how it shoots. You can tell Suzie is impressed. She's dumbstruck and nods, staring. Suzie backs away, amazed. She leaves in awe. She understands now why you can't waste time on exams or anything.

When they come, you know they want to steal your ideas. You realise you should never have let anyone know until your work was finished. You grind your teeth. You've been foolish.

They flick a switch and fill you with their electricity to get rid of yours.

You learn to patch a memory with notions, to juggle hours and listen to ghosts. To be another face and forget what day your birthday is. Your stick bones stab the bed, limbs stripped bald and bare. You stumble over the white, cold tiles with muffled words. You wonder if you'll ever feel warm again.

You spend hours making small, wicker stools. You weave, worry, pick and pluck blue threads into twisted plaits.

In time, you remember the difference between day and night. You learn to watch the sky and follow birds. You notice white flowers nudging aside the dark, each day reaching for light. Your tears surprise you as drops of hope.

You yearn for the sea and air, for the wide horizon and bluest, blue sky. You're hungry for wind and rain. No windows or doors, no metal bars.

After a million cups of tasteless tea, you're allowed to leave.

You walk along the beach and pick up a pearly shell; it looks like an angel's ear fallen out of the pink spring sky. You wonder how old it is, holding nothing inside but a few grains of sand. You listen to the whispering sea while the waves lick your toes. You shut your eyes and throw your head back, remembering that darkest winter. In hospital, you told one of the doctors about the elephants on the beach. You knew he didn't believe you; he nodded and said, 'Hmmm' – like they all did. You jump waves and taste salt on your lips. You enjoy the clean, soft sand blowing against your bare legs in little bites. You take big gulps of fresh air and smile, remembering how much the elephants loved splashing and frolicking in the morning sun. You remember how good it is to be free.

revelation

'You're all very special and God loves each and every one of you,' says Miss Brown. 'Quiet now, children, let's be on our best behaviour. Remember all the things we've practised.'

We tip-toe up to the front two rows in St Theresa's church. This is our last practice for our first Holy Communions. I tell Sophia, 'It's like a wedding day. We have our beautiful white dresses, and everyone fusses over us, but we don't have to have a husband. My big sister says it was her best day ever.'

We take turns going up to the altar to receive a milk chocolate button.

'Pretend this is the Body of Christ you're receiving,' says Miss Brown. She whispers, 'Remember to say "Amen". Don't be in too much of a hurry to swallow the chocolate.'

I know Sophia's dress will be wonderful. She wears clothes from a special shop where they're altered to fit her perfectly. Her dad takes her shopping for clothes. I can't remember ever going shopping with my dad. Sophia's mum and dad are Italian, which makes them different.

'They have funny ways,' my mum says.

Sophia whispers to me on the way out of church, 'Let's practise for our first Holy Communion at my house tomorrow after school.'

'Okay.' I want her to stop talking to me so Miss Brown doesn't tell us off again. Miss Brown is my favourite teacher. She always speaks quietly and has sparkly blue eyes. I hate being told off, but Sophia doesn't care. No matter how much she's shouted at, even when she was sent to the Headmistress. Sister Ignatius put her nose near to hers, and yelled so you could see all her yellow teeth but Sophia didn't blink. I've been told off a lot since being Sophia's best friend.

My mum said last week, 'Any more trouble and I'm going to ask Miss Brown to separate you two.'

Sophia lives in a big house with a pretty mummy and handsome daddy. She doesn't have any brothers or sisters. Sophia has lovely clothes. I get fed up of wearing my sister's clothes. Everything's new and extra fancy at Sophia's house.

Sophia isn't good at taking turns so I allow her to go first with everything. I don't like arguing, it makes my stomach wobble. Sophia pushes Carolyn in the queue at school and calls her Fishface. I know it's not because she smells, it's because she got to be Mary in the Christmas play and Sophia wanted to be. That was months ago, but Sophia never forgets.

Sophia's mummy is always busy on the phone, or talking to her friends in their lovely lounge. I love going to Sophia's house, and in my head I pretend I live there. I touch the long, gold curtains, and sit on the white settee that sinks like marshmallow. I cross my legs and point my toes like film stars do. I stroke the gold cushions that match the curtains. When we have tea, I like the way the knives and forks are shiny on the big glass table, and I like watching the waterfall in the garden. I go to the toilet lots at Sophia's so I can try the different soaps and perfumes. I look at the back of my head as well as the front because there are mirrors everywhere.

It's different at my house.

'Can I take my dress to Sophia's to practise for our first Holy Communion?'

'Certainly not.'

'Please, I'll be really careful, I promise.'

'No. It's to stay hanging up until next Saturday. After your first Communion, you can dress up in it all you want.'

'Sophia's allowed,' I say in a little voice.

'I bet she is,' my mum says. 'She's a spoilt brat.'

I don't want to tell Sophia, but have to. I bite my fingernails and tell her in the playground. 'I'm not allowed to bring my dress to your house.'

'Why not?'

'My mum says I have to keep it nice for Saturday. She says I can dress up in it after our first Communion, so that'll be good, won't it? We could both be princesses.'

'What good is that? Why don't you come and not tell her?'

'I can't.'

'Okay, then.' Sophia flicks her hair back. 'I'll invite Laura instead.' She skips across the playground.

I run after her. 'Wait. Okay, I'll bring it.'

Sophia spins round. 'Great, see you tomorrow.'

I'm not sure what Sophia's mummy does. Sometimes she's upstairs, and sometimes she's down. She spends a lot of time 'getting ready' but I don't know what for. Her daddy has a restaurant and goes there every day to check the waiters and cooks are doing the right thing.

'He can sack them on the spot' – Sophia clicks her fingers – 'like that.'

When I get to Sophia's, her mummy is on the phone, I can hear her laughing. Sophia lets me in and we go straight upstairs.

I carefully pull my Communion dress out of my rucksack. I've put it in a polythene bag to keep it nice. I unfold it gently and lay it flat on Sophia's big bed. I smooth out the creases.

Sophia goes to her massive wardrobe. It goes from one side of the wall to the other. She lifts her Holy Communion dress down. I open my eyes wide. 'Wow, it's like a popped champagne bottle. You know, when it sprays all over.'

'Yes,' she says, stroking it, 'Daddy had it made. It's Italian. It has over three metres of material.'

We strip down to our vests and pants. Then we carefully put the dresses on over our heads. It takes us ages to fasten each other's buttons and tie our sashes.

My dress isn't fancy like Sophia's, but I love it. My nan made it for me so it's extra special. I spin round and round in front of the big, long mirror. I look over my shoulder. 'Oh, I love my dress.'

Sophia's eyebrows meet in the middle in a big V. 'Where did you get it from?'

'My grandma made it for me. That's why it fits so well. Yours is lovely, too,' I tell her quickly, because Sophia's eyes are going little. 'It's very splendid,' I tell her.

Her face turns dark. She looks at herself in the mirror again, and then looks at mine. All of a sudden she spins and throws herself on the bed like a starfish. 'It makes me look fat,' she cries, pulling at the big puffs of material.

'No, it doesn't, it's just got a lot of material.'

'You think I look fat.' Sophia covers her eyes with her hands. 'That's what you're really saying.'

'No, you're not. I didn't say that, I don't think that…'

Sophia cries louder and hits the bed. 'I'm big and ugly.'

I feel hot and red. Sophia is plump because her mummy and daddy allow her to eat anything she wants. She does look fat in her dress. She gets louder and louder.

'Girls, is everything okay up there?' Sophia's mum shouts from the bottom of the stairs.

Sophia sits up. 'Yes, fine, Mama.'

We hold our breath looking at each other, waiting until we hear her high heels clack across the black and white hall floor.

Sophia says, 'I've got an idea, let's put some make-up on. That would make me feel better.'

I nod quickly. 'Yes, let's.'

Sophia puts her finger over her mouth. 'Shh, you wait here.'

I watch her cross the landing and slip into her mum and dad's room. She comes back with a bag bulging full of make-up. 'This will make me feel prettier.' She tips the bag out on the floor; lipsticks, powder, eyeliner, eye shadows and blusher all roll across the floor.

We pick out colours and stand next to each other in front of the mirror. I tell her, 'I've watched my big sister put make-up on lots of times.' The mascara stick smudges again. 'It's harder than it looks, isn't it?'

'My mama can take hours getting ready. I think to do it properly it takes a long time.' Sophia smacks her lips. 'That's what you do when you put lipstick on.'

We rub eye shadow on and off, on and off, until we get the best colour for each of us. When we finish we hold hands in front of the mirror. Sophia looks at herself and then at me. Her mouth turns downwards. 'I think you need more lipstick on.' She picks up the reddest, shiniest lipstick and holds my shoulder. 'Keep still.' She presses round and round my lips. 'There.' She stands back with a big smile. 'See what you think.'

I turn round to look in the mirror, but Sophia goes over on her new Holy Communion shoes that have heels and falls into me. 'Oh, sorry,' she laughs, 'I tripped.'

'It's alright.' I laugh, too. I straighten myself and turn back to the mirror. My mouth drops wide when I see the red running down the middle of my dress. It's like a deep bleeding cut. 'What's happened?'

'Oh golly,' Sophia says, eyes sparkling, 'I had it in my hand when I fell. Soz.'

I run to the bathroom and grab one of the thick, fluffy towels. I don't care if I spoil it. I run the towel under the water and rub my dress hard, trying to sponge the stain out. It smudges and the water turns pink. I scrub and scrub. I start crying. Sophia stands at the door watching me. I stare at her stupid, made-up face. 'You did that on purpose.'

'No, I did not.'

I push past her, pulling my Communion dress off. I bundle it into my bag. I'm so angry my hands are shaking. 'You're jealous of my dress, that's why you did it.'

Sophia throws her head back laughing. 'I would never be jealous of your clothes.'

I run out and down the stairs. I shout up to her, 'I hate you.'

I creep in through the back door at home and straight up to the bathroom. I lock the door and pull my dress out. The stain is like candyfloss all over the front of my beautiful dress. I rub soap over it, trying again to get the stain out. All that happens is the candyfloss gets bigger and bigger.

I unlock the bathroom door after half an hour and wipe my eyes on my sleeve. I carry it downstairs; the dress feels very heavy.

My mum shouts, 'You stupid, naughty girl. I strictly forbade you to take your dress to Sophia's.' She holds it up. 'Look at it, it's ruined.'

I start crying again and think I might be sick. 'I'm never going to be Sophia's friend again.' I hiccup. 'Is there nothing we can do?'

Everyone is cross with me, but the worst is my nan. She isn't angry, but she's sad. She shakes her head. 'After all that hard work I put into it. Dearie me, whatever possessed you?'

Mum puts the whole dress three times in the washing machine. Eventually the stain more or less goes, but the dress is now slightly pink instead of white. There are little bobbles on it after all the washing, and it looks as if it's been worn lots instead of brand new. My eyes water every time I look at it; my dress made completely new just for me, and it's ruined.

'And when Christ's side was pierced, His great love for us gushed out with the mingling of blood and water.'

I listen to the priest and think that what happened to my dress is like being stabbed, it hurts so much.

Laura and Sophia are in the bench behind. They're holding hands, they're best friends now. Sophia's daddy took lots of photos of them outside church. He'll put them up in his restaurant. It will be like being very famous.

The priest says, 'Because God loves us so much He gave his only Son for us to have His flesh and blood.'

I feel a tap on my shoulder and I turn round. Sophia smiles and points down at the bench. I stare at it. I can't believe Sophia would dare do this in God's house. She's scratched *I hate you* into the wood with a golden crucifix she got for her first Holy Communion.

'You're wicked, you'll go to Hell,' I whisper. 'He'll have seen what you've done and He'll punish you.'

Miss Brown leans across from the front bench. 'Shhhh!' She has her finger over her mouth. 'I'm disappointed in you,' she whispers to me. 'After all I told you about behaving, and here you are chattering away.'

I feel my face go red. 'Sorry, Miss.'

I look up at the cross and try to stop crying. I see Jesus with nails in His hands and feet and the blood coming out of His side. I shut my eyes tight thinking how much it must've hurt. I know God is all-powerful. He could make Sophia suffer as much as a crucifixion and even more if He wants. Sophia might burn in Hell forever for such a wicked deed.

I look for my mum and dad, who are somewhere on the other side of church. I find them and make myself smile at them. They stare straight ahead, their mouths are turned downwards. Nan is next to them and looks sad and old. I turn round and see Carolyn and Martha nudging each other. I know they're giggling at my pink dress.

My eyes are prickly. I stare at the cross and the choir starts singing *All Things Bright and Beautiful.* They sound very happy.

I stare at the cross some more, and I understand something very important. I realise Sophia won't get punished for her sins; life isn't fair like that.

I look around the church one more time and feel outside it all.

I try to hold my head up high and sing, but it's too hard, the words get stuck in my throat. I swallow and look away from the cross, because my first Holy Communion day is the day I stop believing in God.

acknowledgements

Thanks to Joseph Higgins for proof reading *Little Crackers* again and again.
Thanks to Tom Higgins for the artwork.
Thanks to Rachel Higgins for the gold stars.
Thanks to Bernard Higgins for time given.
Thanks to Marianne Mitchelson for being wise.
Thanks Anna Woodford – tea helps.
Thanks to Margaret Leahy for letting me write in her lovely house.
Thanks to the Queen's Nursing Institute for raising the bar of good nursing.
Thanks to New Writing North.
Thanks to Iron Press.
Thanks to Craig Hillsley for his detailed editing.
Thank you Sara Hunt for making it easy.

Little Crackers is a work of fiction. Events, places, heroes and villains are imaginary.

about the author

Beda Higgins is an award-winning writer of poetry and prose based in Newcastle. Her first collection of short stories, *Chameleon*, was chosen as a Read Regional Recommendation in 2011. Beda is trained as a general and psychiatric nurse. She is the recipient of two Queen's Nursing Institute Awards and works part time in General Practice.